"Very well, Mr. Carter. I'm going to prove something to you. First I'm going to show you that a Japanese woman who has been properly trained is a match for any American man, and second I'm going to demonstrate that we women in general are not so easily brushed aside."

With that, she unzipped the back of her sundress. "I don't have a *ghi*," she explained, "but there's no one here but the two of us." The dress slipped to the floor and she stepped out of it.

I stiffened. I wasn't sure I liked this. She was pushing things. First getting me down here on some false pretense of taking offense at something I'd said, and now this. I figured either she liked me more than she let on, or there was something else on her mind, and it was this something else that bothered me.

NICK CARTER IS IT!

"Nick Carter out-Bonds James Bond."
                              –Buffalo Evening News

"Nick Carter is America's #1 espionage agent."
                                          –Variety

"Nick Carter is razor sharp suspense."
                                  –King Features

"Nick Carter is extraordinarily big."
                                      –Bestsellers

"Nick Carter has attracted an army of addicted readers . . . the books are fast, have plenty of action and just the right degree of sex . . . Nick Carter is the American James Bond, suave, sophisticated, a killer with both the ladies and the enemy."

Dedicated to the Men of the
Secret Services of the
United States of America

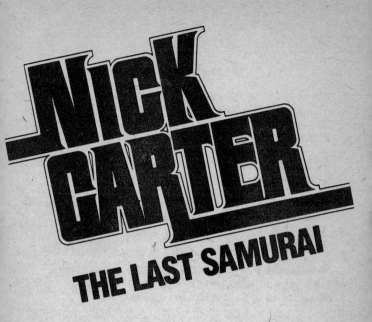

NICK CARTER

THE LAST SAMURAI

CHARTER
NEW YORK

A DIVISION OF CHARTER COMMUNICATIONS INC
A GROSSET & DUNLAP COMPANY
51 Madison Avenue
New York, New York 10010

THE LAST SAMURAI

One

I opened the heavy steel door to the gymnasium and looked inside. There was a broad expanse of highly polished floor; wrestling mats quilted with oblongs of sunlight were scattered about; and in one corner stood some tumbling equipment. But there was no sign anywhere of Gigi Minamoto, the Japanese girl I was supposed to meet here.

It wasn't an important date, just a silly sort of bet we'd had, and I toyed with the idea of leaving. But then I thought better of it. After all, here I was in my *ghi* already, and I could always use the workout. So I went in, slipped off my shoes, and placed them next to one of the mats. Then I began the slow, snakelike movements of the Tai Chi cycle. I hadn't gotten more than a few minutes into the warm-up when I heard the door slam behind me.

"Hi," she said brightly, and when I turned she was bent over, unstrapping a sandal, her thick black hair hanging like a curtain from her head almost to the floor. "I'm not so awfully late, am I?"

"Not so awfully, no."

"Good." She walked barefoot across the glistening boards onto the mat where I was standing. "I'm a little surprised to see you," she went on. "I guess I didn't really think you'd come." She stood directly in front of me and for the first time I noticed how small she was—I guessed about five-two—and yet perfectly proportioned, with a springy, athletic grace to her movements.

"I don't like it when people infer I'm a male chauvinist. Especially when all I did was make a simple statement of fact."

"You said women don't belong in martial arts competition with men. And when I said I was as good as you in any art you care to name, you scoffed."

"I didn't scoff."

"Maybe you didn't say it, but I saw it in your look. You don't think I could best you."

"I never said . . ."

"No, admit it. You don't think I could, do you? I mean, if we really tried, if we were both fighting for our lives, you don't think I could win."

"You're right. I guess I don't."

"Very well, Mr. Carter. I'm going to prove something to you. First I'm going to show you that a Japanese woman who has been properly trained is a match for any American man. And second I'm going to demonstrate that we women in general are not so easily brushed aside."

With that, she unzipped the back of her sundress. "I don't have a *ghi*," she explained, "but there's no one here except for the two of us." The dress slipped to the floor and she stepped out of it.

If she was attractive dressed, nude she was positively breath-taking. Long, sinuous arms, high breasts that looked up at you alertly, eagerly; tight, well-conditioned thighs disappearing into a perfect v behind the flimsy veil of a pair of blue lace bikini panties, the only article of clothing she still wore.

She watched me watching her. "If you have a *ghi* and I don't," she went on, breaking into my thoughts, "then I have the advantage."

"You want me to take my clothes off, too?"

"It would be fairer. That way I wouldn't have anything to grab onto."

I stiffened. I wasn't sure I liked this. She was pushing things. First getting me down here on some false pretense of taking offense at something I'd said, and now this. I figured either she liked me more than she let on, or there was something else on her mind, and it was this something else that bothered me. When you make your living working undercover, you learn to be cautious.

I'd known this girl only a week. She was a therapist here at the AXE rest and recuperation facility outside Phoenix. I'd checked into the facility a few days ago after a stint in the hospital for a dislocated shoulder I'd gotten during my last assignment. She'd been tending to it, kneading it mostly, and massaging it. Now I know the security people in this place are the best there are, and that the checks they run on perspective employees are stringent, but still I wondered.

And yet as I looked down at her, her breasts trembling slightly as she took a breath, I knew I wanted her. I decided I'd take my chances. I untied my tunic and took it off, then my pants. At this point I had nothing left but my jock strap.

"We might as well go the whole route," I said, slipping that off and tossing it aside.

"Okay." She rolled the panties down her thighs and kicked them off the mat with her foot, revealing between her thighs a tiny triangle of baby-fine black hair so ephemeral an artist might have air-brushed it on. "This is the way we fight in Japan," she said.

She made me a curt bow, which was only slightly comical and all the more engaging considering she didn't have stitch on, then doubled her fists and assumed *hachiji-dachi*, the basic karate stance. I shook my head and did the same. I guessed that if I wanted her, I was going to have to first go through this charade of a fight.

We broke stance and circled one another, not quite knowing how to start. Neither of us wanted to be the first to make contact. Then out of the blue she rushed me, thrusting her foot into my stomach in a long frontal kick. It was only half-hearted and I managed to catch her by the ankle and pull up. She fell down hard and stayed down, looking up at me with a mixture of surprise and indignation.

I didn't say anything but I watched her expression, hoping for a smile or some hint that she was going to take this little setback lightly, but the smile never came. Instead, she sat there glaring up at me, and if there was any element of joking around about all this, if there had been any hope of dismissing the whole thing as a girlish prank, it was gone now. She meant business.

She rolled to one side and kicked again from a crouch position. It was an unusual attack and I wasn't ready. Luckily, I got a forearm in the way, but this was no faint-hearted kick. She stung my arm, then skipped away before I could counterattack.

She was up now, dancing tauntingly in front of me. Only this time it was my turn. I rushed her with a series of kicks and punches, trying to unseat her, to disturb her balance.

But hitting her was like hitting a brick wall. She defended herself against each blow and never moved a half-step in either direction. Finally, on my last punch I caught her chin with my elbow. I could tell it hurt her.

I backed off to see if she wanted to give up and call it quits, but she didn't give me any sign. Her jaw set determinedly, she wasn't looking at me. Down deep, I really didn't think she'd had enough, and in a way I hoped she hadn't. As they used to say down on Delaney Street, this kid's got moxie.

I squared off for another attack, but if I thought that last blow had slowed her any, I was wrong. As I came toward her, she grabbed my hair, fell down, and flipped me high into the air—and I landed squarely onto my dislocated shoulder. It didn't hurt all that much—it was mostly healed—but the unexpected pain kept me lying on the mat a split second. Then I quickly pulled myself together and tried to scramble to my feet, knowing she'd be looking for just such an opening. But she was faster than I thought. Two swift kicks knocked my legs out from under me and sent me sprawling.

Then she danced away, letting me get up un-molested. Apparently she enjoyed this bit of toying with me, and I let her have her little victory.

We came together warily in the middle of the mat. By this time we'd each inflicted a little damage—and we knew enough to be careful.

We circled. I moved my hands hypnotically in front of her face, hoping to distract her long enough to give me an opening. Her eyes flickered away from mine, and I saw my chance. With a yell, I leapt into the air and thrust my foot into her stomach. It's a classic move—known as *yoko-tobi-geri*—and it caught her unaware.

I'd hoped to knock the wind out of her and get this thing over with quickly, but no chance. Even though I made clean contact with her practically unprotected abdomen, she rolled with the blow beautifully, letting her entire body absorb the shock. Her stomach muscles were as firm as the underbelly of an Icelandic cod.

She hit the mat and rolled, then sprang to her feet. I couldn't help but be impressed. The measure of any karate champion is "hara," or balance. One asks: How well is he rooted? Can he be upset, caught by surprise, moved? If he can't, then he's firm in his purpose in life and undefeatable in battle. Gigi Minamoto had this elusive quality in abundance. As much as any man I'd ever fought.

She charged me again, peppering me with fast jabs and kicks from both feet. I stood my ground, countering each one as fast as she could deliver them, and, on my last counter punch, popped her neatly on the nose, not enough to bloody it, but hard enough to let her know I could have if I'd wanted to.

She backed off a minute, holding her nose and blinking. She looked at me strangely; I wasn't sure what she was thinking except she wasn't as mad at me anymore.

She side-stepped toward me, ready to engage me again, only this time passively, waiting for me to attack. I obliged with a fast punch I really had no hope of landing. She grabbed my arm and braced for another judo throw, only this time I was ready. I shifted my weight, and instead of catapulting head over heels, we simply tumbled onto the mat in a pile.

Then it became a wrestling match, each of us trying to hold the smooth, sweat-soaked limbs of the other. I was caught up in it. I wanted to dominate her.

Finally, I succeeded in straddling her, pinning her wrists to the mat.

She was a strong girl, and holding her took a great deal of strength. I watched as she struggled to get free, beautiful even now, face dripping with sweat, the muscles of her neck straining as she wrenched her head from side to side.

Then she stopped fighting suddenly and looked at me. Our eyes met and I could feel her body go limp underneath me. I started to say something, then stopped. I knew what she was thinking. We were both thinking it.

I let go of her wrists and her arms entwined behind my head and pulled my face down to hers. We kissed for what seemed a long time. This was where our fight had been leading us all along, I thought.

I rolled off her and lay down to one side, sliding my hand down her body. She trembled like a child. At that moment she was completely defenseless. The sweat allowed my hand to glide effortlessly over her skin. I brushed between her legs.

"Yes," she said softly in my ear.

A few minutes later I was drowning in her.

When it was over we lay for a time without moving. Then she rolled me off her and stood up. She shook out her long black hair and walked to the other side of the mat.

"Where are you going?" I asked.

"I have to leave." She'd found her underwear and was stepping into them, her back to me.

"Just like that?"

"Isn't that the way you men like to do things? Wham, bam, thank you ma'am?"

I got up and approached her from behind. "I don't get it," I said, putting my hand softly on her shoulder. "This was a very nice thing that happened here. Let's not spoil it . . ."

She turned around and looked at me sharply. "How?

By getting all emotional? No, I didn't mean that. I'm sorry. I really have to go. This isn't the way it was supposed to turn out.''

"How was it supposed to turn out?''

She didn't answer me. She had her dress on now and was zipping it. "I'm sorry, Nick. I didn't mean for it to happen like this.''

Before I could stop her, she'd picked up her sandals and run out the door. I wasn't sure, but I thought she was crying.

After the door slammed, it was just me and a lot of unanswered questions in the big room of the gymnasium. I gathered my clothes together and dressed slowly, thinking.

I wasn't sure why she'd reacted the way she did, and it bothered me. Was there some other motive in all this beside just seducing me? Maybe things hadn't gone as planned. I didn't know, but I learned long ago that, when it comes to women, it's best not to think too much and to wait.

I didn't have much time for thinking anyway. When I got back to my room, I found a message shoved under the door. Hawk wanted to see me in Washington at once.

*   *   *

As I walked into Hawk's office, he was standing with his back to me, his hands in the pockets of his baggy pants, staring out the window. It was July in Washington and ungodly hot, but he wore his suit jacket just as always: summer, winter, or nuclear holocaust. I started to say something clever, but thought better of it. From the look on his face, he wasn't in a joking mood.

"You here finally?'' he said, turning around.

"I came as fast as I could."

"All right. Sit down. We've got an emergency." He settled in behind the big, beat-up wooden desk and opened a file folder. I pulled up a chair.

"Know anything about recombinant genetics?" he asked.

"Sort of. You can rearrange the genes in a cell. Some people say you can create anything you want."

"That's right, organisms that never existed before."

"Diseases without cures," I said.

He looked at me levelly as if trying to decide if that was a flip answer, and if he was going to tolerate it if it was. "Whether you know it or not, that's exactly what's happened. About three weeks ago some scientists at the University of Michigan were trying to synthesize interferon. They think it might be a cure for cancer. The idea is they rearrange genes in certain bacteria and the bacteria produce the chemical. At least that's the idea. But something went wrong and a new organism popped up, and this thing, whatever it is, likes to eat green vegetable matter. In fact, it consumes leaves, grass, trees, anything green so fast they tell me one plateful could strip the entire planet bare in a matter of months."

"The entire planet?"

"I was talking to the Bureau liaison last night. That's what he said."

Jesus, I thought. No wonder the old man's gruff. He hates getting anything secondhand from the F.B.I. "That sounds incredible," I said.

"I know. It's hard to believe, but fifteen years ago we said the same thing about Agent Orange."

"The entire planet. That's amazing. I don't suppose they've developed an antidote for it either."

"It can be killed. That's not the problem. The problem is, it's airborne and it multiplies at an incredible rate. Once it's loose, you could never contain it."

"Let's hope it never gets loose."

"As a matter of fact, Killmaster, that's exactly why you're here. Yesterday, one of the culture dishes they use to grow this stuff—they're calling it MBD, microbiological defoliant—turned up missing. So far we've managed to keep a lid on it, but if this stuff isn't found soon, word's going to get out."

"There'll be panic. And the Bureau's handling it? Who's the agent in charge?"

"Bill Hagarty."

I shook my head. "Never heard of him."

"He's young. I don't know. I don't think they've had the slightest idea what they're doing over there since Hoover died."

"What I want to know is, if this thing is only one day old, and the Bureau is just warming up on it, why are we being called in?"

He threw the file folder across the desk to me. "Lo Sin was in the area."

"Lo Sin? That's impossible."

"Apparently not. He was seen checking into a motel in the Ann Arbor area. He spent the night, then left in a hurry."

"But it couldn't have been Lo Sin. He was abandoned by his guides high in the mountains. There's no way he could have gotten down alive."

"Apparently he did, N-3. We have a positive identification on this."

I opened the file. Inside was a timetable of the stakeout on Lo Sin's motel. I read it over quickly and noticed there were several hours of the second day unaccounted for.

"You have to admit this defoliant business is in keeping with the Buck-Rogers-twenty-first-century sort of thing that appeals to Lo Sin," Hawk said, watching me and drumming his fingers.

"Yes, but it's out of his league."

"That's what makes it such a concern. I wouldn't want to hang the world in a balance against Lo Sin's greed. The world would lose."

I closed the folder and pushed it back up on the desk. "When do I leave?"

"Immediately. We've got you booked on a three forty-five flight. You'll be using the cover, Nick Carstons, Amalgamated Press. The local office knows you're coming. Hagarty's been briefed, too. He thinks you're CIA. No reason why he should know any different. Good luck and keep me posted."

Two

If it weren't for forty-odd thousand college kids, Ann Arbor would be just another sleepy Midwestern city entrenched in mechanism-like routines that go back generations. But the students manage to break up the monotony. Everywhere you look there are multitudes of scrubbed, smiling faces and heads of chestnut and blond, ungrayed hair. All in all, it's about the last place you'd expect to find the beginning of the end of the world.

I got to the Holiday Inn around supper time, checked in, then went down to meet Bill Hagarty in the lounge. He was already seated at a table waiting for me. When he saw me, he got up and extended his hand.

"Bill Hagarty," he said.

"Nicholas Carstons. 'Nick' to my friends."

"I hope we'll be friends, Nick." From the way he said it, I gathered he didn't have too many at the moment. His handshake was a little damp and I could see he'd already had several drinks.

"Sit down. What're you drinking?"

"Scotch."

"Scotch," he told the bartender. "Make it a double, and I'll have another brandy."

We waited in silence while the drinks were made. When Hagarty had a fresh glass in front of him, he started to fill me in on where things stood.

"I'm going to be brutally honest about this," he said, fingering the little cocktail napkin under his drink. "We don't have much in the way of leads. Security in that laboratory is non-existent. It was probably an inside job, but we can't be sure. We've been checking out the personnel who had access to the area where the culture was kept, and so far everybody looks guilty."

He waited for me to say something, and when I didn't, he went on. "It happened the night before last, some time between ten and three in the morning. We know it was after ten because that's when Dr. Meade— the big honcho out there—went home, and he says he checked it, and that it was after three because that's when it was reported missing."

"Anybody in the lab between those hours?"

"Two. Dr. Neil Strommond and an assistant, a Miss Trumbull."

"Any possibility there?"

"As easily as anyone else. We're still checking them out. But I don't have much hope for it."

"Didn't they hear anything? Notice anything suspicious?"

"You'd think they would, wouldn't you? This lab isn't that big a place. You'll see for yourself when we go out there tomorrow. Just a cinder block building out in the middle of nowhere. You'd think a strange noise or something would've alerted them. They'd know right away if someone was in the building. But these scientific types are amazing. When they're working on something, they're in a fog. You can't break through, even when you're talking with them.''

"Are you sure?'' I asked. "Maybe they weren't working at all. Maybe there's something going on between the good doctor and his lady assistant.''

This idea amused him. He shook his head. "They say they were working in separate rooms, and I believe it. You really have to know these people to understand. They live in a world of their own.''

He took a long pull at his drink and almost drained it. Then he put it back on the table and looked at the glass distractedly as he rolled it back and forth on its edge.

"They've been driving me nuts, too,'' he went on. "It's like they don't know what they've done. Here they go and discover the most potent weapon of the century, something so dangerous just to drop it spells the end of everything, and what do they do? They squabble among themselves over who owns what until they fumble the ball and lose it. Then they sit me down and try and convince me just how dangerous and valuable this stuff they just lost really is.''

He stopped talking and in the dim light of the bar I could see how young he was—not more than twenty-eight—even though as he stared into his glass there was a deep furrow of concern across his forehead that aged him considerably.

"Maybe this time we've really blown it,'' he said. "I work in government. I see how things are bungled and screwed up. The hopes of mankind, our chances for survival, misfiled, misappropriated, squandered. Maybe it was just inevitable. Sooner or later we were bound to come up with something so dangerous, so destructive, that mishandling it would kill us all. Then we'd be a lead pipe cinch to let it slip through our fingers."

He finished what was left in his glass and set it down with a clack. "I drink too much." He stood up none too steadily and began fumbling in his pocket.

"Don't worry about it," I told him. "I'll take care of it."

He stopped fumbling and looked at me. "Okay. I owe you one, then." He made a sticky sound with his mouth and looked around the empty bar, trying to focus.

"You going to be able to make it home?"

"Don't worry about me," he said. "I'll pick you up in the morning. Eight o'clock."

I nodded. He turned awkwardly and I watched as he threaded his way between the tables and out the door.

*   *   *

He still looked a little rough the next morning when he came to get me in his car. His eyes were red and his razor hand must have been a little shaky. In the clear light of day he looked more his age.

On the way we talked about unimportant things and the conversation lapsed a good deal. I got the feeling he didn't want to discuss the night before, so we didn't. Instead I watched the Michigan countryside slide by the window and tried to imagine what it would look like without green plants.

We drove for twenty minutes or more. Hagarty had said this place was isolated, but I'd had no idea just what an out-of-the-way spot it was until we came over a hill into what looked to be a completely deserted valley. There were no houses or farms, and no signs of human life. Even the land was unfenced. At the bottom of the hill we took a turn into a gravel driveway that extended back behind a copse of pines. This led to a parking lot in front of a squat, nondescript, one-story building. At the front door, wearing a white lab coat unbuttoned in front, stood a slender, bearded man in his mid-forties, apparently waiting for us. He walked over as soon as we were stopped.

"Dr. Meade, this is Nick Carstons," Hagarty said by way of introducing us. Meade shook my hand and adjusted his glasses. He looked as though he hadn't slept in a week.

"Carstons," he said, as though he were trying to place me. "You'll have to excuse me, but I've met so many people in the last few days and I can't seem to remember who they are or what they do."

"You don't know me, Doctor. I just got here. All I want to do is look the place over and have you tell me what happened."

"I see. All right." From his tone it was obvious he'd already told his story more times than he could count and didn't relish having to tell it again.

He led us into the building, through a heavy metal door into a small lobby. There was nothing in this room but an empty glass case on the wall and a fire extinguisher. From the lobby a narrow corridor ran straight back to another which ran perpendicular. Off the second corridor was a total of eight small rooms. Meade stopped in each one of them, flipped on the lights, and told us what went on there. Each room had its quota of lab tables, electronic equipment, and experimental animals that made a racket whenever they smelled humans.

"Where is everybody?" I asked after the third or fourth empty room.

"I told them not to come in today. Was that all right?"

"Fine, Doc," said Hagarty. "As long as we know where they all are."

Meade took us into the next room and opened the door. "And this is the storage area," he said, turning on the light. This room was larger than the rest. There was a bank of shelves against one wall; against the other stood a sink with water running in it and a big, double-door refrigerator. The water in the drain made an unhealthy gurgling sound.

"This is where the *e coli* are stored after they've been treated. Then we take the cultures in for viewing under the electron microscope on campus."

"Isn't that a little inconvenient?" I asked. "Why don't you have a microscope here?"

"Ectectron microscopes are not easy to come by, Mr. Carstons. They require funding and funding is something we're a little short of lately."

He walked to the refrigerator door and opened it. "The MBD culture was kept here on the second shelf. I checked it at ten o'clock Monday night. It was gone when Strommond checked it again before he went home at three."

I bent down to examine the shelf. It was empty now; obviously Hagarty's team had taken it out and put it through every possible test. Then I checked over the outside of the refrigerator. "There's no lock on this door," I said.

"We never thought there was a need for one. We're scientists, not criminals." From the edge in Meade's voice I gathered I wasn't the first to make this observation. I was beginning to understand why no one could say for sure if someone had broken in or not.

"But something that valuable," I persisted. "Wouldn't you keep it under lock and key?"

"Value is a relative term, Mr. Carstons. Remember,

we didn't go out looking for this discovery. We came upon it by accident. What we are trying to do is expedite the synthesis of a chemical which we have every reason to believe will be a great benefit to mankind. And in trying to do that, we stumbled on something that may very well kill us all. You can understand why we weren't pleased.''

''Wait a minute. You didn't like this stuff, so you deliberately left it out where anybody could take it, hoping they'd get rid of it for you?''

''That's not what I said . . .''

Hagarty, who'd apparently already covered these points with Meade before and was now nosing around the room, presently bumped into a tray of what looked like sheep gut in the sink. When Meade heard it, he sprang to it defensively.

''Don't touch that!'' he said. ''That's a new method of extracting the *e colis*.'' He pushed Hagarty out of the way and readjusted the apparatus, balancing it back and forth until he had it the way he wanted. ''Maybe we ought to finish this discussion in my office. It'll be easier to talk.''

Meade's office was just up the hall, a modest room barely large enough for a desk and two chairs. The two of them sat; I volunteered to stand.

Hagarty began asking questions about the other men on the research team, trying to get some hint as to how they all felt about one another. It was a good ploy, although Meade was obviously unwilling to play the gossip. I listened, but after a while my mind began to wander.

It wasn't much of an office. Certainly no one was ever going to accuse Dr. Meade of expropriating funds from his project for his own use. There was a bookshelf in one corner crammed with books and pamphlets, and

snapshots were scotchtaped to one wall. On the other
wall was a bulletin board stuck with a multitude of
papers. On the bulletin board I spied a list of names.

"What's this?" I asked Meade.

"A roster of the students in my seminar."

"Graduate students?"

"Yes."

"Would any of these have access to the lab?"

"They don't have keys, if that's what you mean.
They've all been out here at one time or another. They
know the routine. But surely you don't think—these
students are reputable people. They've come a long
way to get in this class."

"What is it?" Hagarty asked. I handed him the list.
He looked it over, then set it on the desk in front of
Meade. "We have that already," he said.

I pointed out to Meade the name that had caught my
eye. "What about this one?"

"Thao Seng? He's a Chinese boy. Very bright, but
then most of them are. Quiet. Keeps to himself. Surely
just because he's Chinese you don't think—"

"He's definitely Chinese?"

"No. He's Taiwanese, actually. I remember that
specifically because he was so upset when our government recognized mainland China."

It fit. Or it might fit. A disgruntled student in a
foreign country was just the sort of recruit Lo Sin would
be looking for. There was an address next to the name:
110 Clermont Street, Apartment 20.

"May I have a copy of this?" I asked.

"Take that. I have others."

I folded it and put it in my pocket.

The interview with Meade had run into rough water.
Hagarty asked several more questions, but the good
doctor was reluctant to commit himself. Finally,

Hagarty told him to suspend operations at the lab until further notice, and we left.

On the way back to town Hagarty asked to see the list again. He unfolded it and read it while he was driving. "Which one were you looking at?" he asked.

I pointed to the name, Thao Seng.

He handed it back to me. "I talked to that kid myself. He's a dead end. He's . . . what's that word they use to describe the Chinese? Inscrutable. He was inscrutable. But he's a dead end anyway."

"Why's that?"

"He was out of town somewhere when it happened. Chicago, I think."

"He still might have had something to do with it. I'd like to talk to him all the same."

"Suit yourself. But I'll tell you what I'm betting on. I'm betting one of these effete-intellectual-snob doctors dumped this stuff to keep it out of the hands of the Pentagon. I'll lay you ten to one, that's what happened."

"Maybe."

Traffic picked up as we neared the city. Hagarty dropped me at my motel, then headed on downtown to his office after telling me he'd get a hold of me later.

I went in immediately and rented a car. Then I headed for Clermont Street.

Three

Clermont Street was two and a half blocks of dirty wooden houses facing each other over a strip of broken pavement about three miles from the university campus. Number one hundred and ten sat in a state of disrepair just before the road dead-ended into a railyard.

I pulled up in front of the house and checked the sheet again. One hundred and ten was the right number and the numerals were on the porch railing, even though they'd been painted over years before. Yet the place looked deserted. Waist-high weeds stood in the yard; windows were boarded up or broken.

I turned off the car and went up the walk to the porch. There were no bells to ring, but I laid a hand against the dusty wooden door and it opened.

Inside, the vestibule was dark and smelled of decaying wood. I listened, and thought I heard movement upstairs. A long series of mailboxes on the wall were empty except for one, which had a small white card with the name Thao Seng typed on it. It looked fresh.

I climbed the staircase and found a dark hallway at the top, so dark in fact that I had to *feel* the numbers on the doors until I found the one I was looking for. I knocked. Nothing. I knocked again and waited. Then suddenly the door sprang open and there stood a long-haired Chinese youth in tennis shoes and a tee shirt. He seemed very surprised to see me.

I was just about to say something when he turned abruptly and ran back into the apartment. I stood there for a split second, then took off after him.

He disappeared through a door in the kitchen. There was a stairwell that I guessed led down to the basement. It was steep and dark, too dark to be sure he wasn't waiting for me a little further down with a weapon; I pulled Wilhelmina, my 9mm Luger, out of her hard leather case under my arm and proceeded with caution.

On the first landing were two doors. One led to the first floor apartment, the other was a rear ground-level exit. Both were wedged tight and I didn't think he'd gone through either of them, or I'd have heard him. Just then there was a noise downstairs.

One wall of the staircase to the basement was cement foundation, the other open. I pressed my back against the cement and side-stepped on down, Wilhelmina out, ready for anything.

When I reached the bottom, I waited. There was a whirring noise, like a small electric motor running. It was curious. I couldn't place it. I squinted, but I couldn't see a thing.

The longer I waited, the less I liked it. I had the distinct impression coming down here was a big mistake.

I felt along the wall for a light switch, but I didn't get

far. Suddenly a blunt object hit my hand. Before I could pull it back, another something, like the blunt end of a hard-swung hammer, hit the other hand and Wilhelmina dropped to the floor.

I stooped to retrieve her and got hit with the same thing again, only this time I knew what it was. From the smell of leather it was a boot, and whoever it belonged to, he wasn't the long-haired, tennis-shoe-clad kid I'd chased down here.

I needed some fighting room, so I took the blow and rolled with it, ending up face down against a pile of wet cardboard boxes.

I jumped to my feet. My hands stung from where they'd been hit, but they didn't hurt so badly that I couldn't do some damage in return. The only problem was how. Although my eyes had adjusted to the darkness I still couldn't see anything clearly.

I sensed him moving to my right and I charged, putting up a wall of karate punches and kicks he'd be damned hard pressed to get away from. I caught him several times, once neatly on the chin, I knew, because I could feel his head snap back. I moved to close in on that spot with an old-fashioned right hook when my hand hit something solid. It felt like a car door. The knuckles of my hand cracked sickeningly and a bolt of pain shot up my arm. Was that his arm? I wondered.

I didn't get much time to mull this over. The next thing I knew he was using my head for a punching bag; hands, arms, elbows, all feeling like they were wrapped in cement. My knees buckled and I went down. Then he started kicking my chest and stomach, hoping to do internal damage.

He was a real pro about it, though. He knew just how far to push it. He'd stopped me pretty good, then backed off, leaving me on the floor not quite out. Then he rolled me over with his foot, triggering the spring release for Hugo, the pencil-thin stiletto, I keep in a chamois case on my forearm. Hugo ejected, but my hand wasn't there to catch him, and he skittered off across the floor.

My mystery assailant then wedged another toe under my shoulder and tried to roll me over face down. But he'd miscalculated: I wasn't as incapacitated as he thought. I grabbed his foot, gave it a shove, and he went tumbling into the darkness with a crash.

I dragged myself to my feet and hobbled off, looking for some kind of shelter. I had no intention of fighting any more; I knew when to retreat. But I had something else in my mind. Whoever this tough guy was he was waiting down here for one specific reason: to hurt me badly. And I wanted to know who he was and why me.

I found a darker patch of the basement which luckily turned out to be a niche of some kind. I ducked into it and leaned back against the wall to rest for a second. I knew I didn't have much time. I had only one weapon left, Pierre, the tiny gas bomb which I keep where no personal search will ever find it, in a sack next to my scrotum. Pierre was my last hope.

Round and smooth, about the size of a pullet egg, Pierre was designed with a very specific talent. He was meant to be used in small confined areas where one wants to stun but not kill. He isn't much good out in the open where the gas dissipates, and he certainly isn't any good in a tiny basement where the thrower can't avoid being gassed himself. But I've found over the years that Pierre can be far more versatile if one is willing to get to know him. I unscrewed his case. There are really two bombs. In one half is the nerve gas itself, oily, smelly, and in this concentration, deadly. In the other is the propellant, a sodium chlorate compound which is highly volatile in water. I removed the plastic membrane that separates the two halves and put the one containing the nerve gas carefully on the floor. He was getting to his feet, I could hear him grunting. In a moment he'd come looking for me.

I chucked the chlorate crystals on the floor. My hope was that there would be enough moisture there for them to react, though not explosively. Sure enough, they started to sputter and smoke and a dull light filled the room.

He stood about ten feet from me, looking at the glowing chlorate in amazement. He was short, definitely Oriental, wearing a dark suit that looked two sizes too small. He had an enormous chest and back for his size, so big that he strained the button of his jacket; but by far the most peculiar part of him was his head. It was shaved and the skin of it was practically translucent. Blue veins ran beneath the scalp and on either temple were large lumps of what looked like scar-tissue. He looked up and saw me staring from my niche just as the light was beginning to fail.

I dove for the floor. In the last seconds I'd seen where Wilhelmina had fallen when she'd been knocked out of my hand. If I could get her back, I could tip the scales in my direction.

I scrambled, but the beating I'd taken earlier slowed me down. He lashed out with a kick that caught me in the stomach. I curled like a worm in a fire. From the sound of it, he'd broken a rib. He hit me a few more times, and thankfully I lost consciousness.

When I came to, I was groggy and in a great deal of pain. When I slowly pulled myself to my feet I found that I couldn't stand completely up. For a minute I just stood there doubled over.

Then I groped for the stairs, found them, and took my time climbing to the first landing. The rear exit door was open, but the door to the first floor apartment was still wedged tight. I banged on it, thinking by some miracle someone might answer, but nothing happened.

I climbed to the second floor, stopping once along the way to get my breath. Every time I inhaled, a fire started in my side and after a while I had to wait a few minutes until the fire subsided.

The door to the kitchen of the second floor apartment stood open. The apartment was dark. I'd gotten here in the early afternoon; it was now twilight. I guessed I must have lay on the basement floor five, maybe six hours.

I turned on the light. The kitchen was empty, except for some rags and sheets of newspaper that looked as though they might have been used as shelfpaper eons ago. There was no stove or refrigerator.

The front room was the same story. No furniture, no carpeting, no drapes. The place looked like it had been stripped, or never furnished in the first place. There must have been something here the first time I came through, I thought. But I was moving so fast I couldn't say for certain.

I went into the bedrooms. They were empty, as well, although not completely. On the floor of one I found a plastic case, the sort that movie film might come in. I stooped down with some effort and put it in my pocket. Then I left.

Outside, the cool Michigan breeze stirred the night air, and a few deep breaths did me more good than a medicine chest full of pills.

I drove back to the motel, still hurting. I had to hold the wheel with one hand and my side with the other.

When I made it upstairs to my room, I heard the

phone ringing. I took my time answering. I knew who it had to be.

"Where the hell have you been all day?" Hagarty's booming voice wanted to know from the other end of the line. "I've been trying to get a hold of you."

"Talking with Thao Seng."

"That boy must be quite a conversationalist. But it doesn't matter anyway. The mystery is solved. The defoliant's been found."

"Found?"

"Not found, exactly, but we know what happened to it. Strommond confessed about three hours ago. He took it and destroyed it that night in the lab. He says he did it for the sake of mankind. How about that for a kick in the head? Nick? You still there?"

"I'm here. Listen, Bill, did you check his story out carefully?"

"We're still working on it. It was his girl friend, the Trumbull woman, who put us on to it. She thinks he's some kind of hero. At any rate, this thing is a long ways from over. That was a federally funded project, and strictly speaking that defoliant was government property. The Justice Department is already talking about prosecuting."

"And they'll make a national figure out of Strommond in the process. Are you certain he's the one who did it? Absolutely sure?"

"Reasonably. We aren't finished with it yet, but everything fits so far. Why? You got some reason to believe he didn't?"

"Just a hunch. I could be wrong."

"You want to share it with me?"

"Not right now. It's not much of a lead." I lied to him. None of what he was telling me made any sense, but I wasn't sure I wanted Hagarty to know that.

"Suit yourself. If you want to stay on here, that's up to you," he said, "but the Bureau's going to be pulling out. We'll do the pretrial, of course, but that might not be for months."

"My agency isn't as structured as all that."

"I know. If you need anything just holler."

"All right. Thanks." I hung up and an eerie feeling descended over me. If Strommond had really done what he'd said, and there had been no one else involved, then what was this episode in the basement of 110 Clermont Street? It was like a piece to a completely different puzzle.

I took the phone book out of the top drawer of the nightstand and started calling local doctors, beginning with the letter "A" and working through the list. It took me six calls to find one who'd come to the motel.

After I talked to him, I lay back on the bed to wait. I wondered what kind of man Strommond would have to be to take credit for something like this if he hadn't done it. What was the motive? Notoriety? By the time the newspapers and the other media were done, his name would be a household word. It must be tough making a reputation these days, at least in the high-powered circles he probably traveled in, and not a bad image to leave in the public mind either, Saviour of the world. Ms. Trumbull would no doubt wait for him faithfully all the months he was in prison.

It took twenty minutes for the doctor to get there. He was young, with icy hands. He looked me over, asking a lot of questions. I told him it was a bar fight. He wasn't completely satisfied, but as long as there were no knife wounds or bullet holes, he saw no reason to say anything. He patched me up, taped my ribs, and wrote me out a prescription. Then he put a couple of extra rolls of tape on the nightstand and left. After he was gone, I fell into a much-needed sleep.

I woke up late the next morning to the sound of a key being put in the lock. The door swung open just as I rose off the bed to see who it was, and I stood there staring at the maid, a high-school girl in a plain linen dress with a cart full of cleaning aids behind her. From the look on her face, I could guess the impression I made.

"I'm sorry," she said. "There was no sign on the door. . . ."

"That's all right. Come back later."

She started to leave, then stopped and looked around the door at me. "Are you okay?" she asked.

"I'm fine. Don't worry. The doctor's already been here."

She nodded, then for a brief second just stared, and I knew my face must have been a sight.

The harsh light in the bathroom proved me right. Even though a lot of the swelling had gone down, the skin was still split in several places and the bruises made it look as though someone had tried to push me head first through a meat grinder.

I got the styptic pencil out of my dop kit and did the best I could, then dressed and went downstairs to the parking lot. The tape on my ribs helped support the bone and kept it from aching. Though it didn't make it any easier to breathe, it did make it possible to walk.

I let myself down easily into the car seat. As long as I didn't move too fast, I was all right. I started the engine and headed back to the house. I wanted to see 110 Clermont in the light of day.

I made a left at the corner and came down Clermont between the dilapidated houses I'd seen the day before. Only when I got to the place I was looking for, what I saw was enough to bring me up short in the middle of the street. The broken-down unpainted two story box of a building I'd been in yesterday was no more. In its place was a heap of broken boards in an open foundation. In short it had been reduced to toothpicks. The wrecking crew sat on the curb having lunch.

I parked and walked over. The foreman, a meaty old man who looked as though he really enjoyed tearing buildings apart, talked with me for a few minutes, but wasn't very helpful. He worked for a company, that worked for a company that worked for an outfit known as Landmark Realty. And Landmark Realty, I figured, was a dead end.

At any rate, he said the destruction order had been in the works for months, but he had no idea why they chose this particular day to do it.

I told him I was an antique dealer interested in old buildings. Then I asked if I could look the place over. He agreed and I thanked him.

I walked down the sidewalk and up the front steps. There was no house attached to them. The porch just hung in mid air like a stage prop. Beyond it was the bare foundation, nothing more than a big concrete box in the ground. I let myself down into it carefully and began to kick through the rubble. It was a good twenty minutes before I found Wilhelmina lying on the damp floor. She needed oiling, but other than that was in good shape.

Hugo was a little more difficult to locate. He'd slipped under the door of what had used to be a coal bin. I had to break off a support rod and use that to pry the door up to get to him.

But the two weapons were all I found. Any evidence of the battle I'd fought or of the mysterious Oriental who'd done so much damage to me had been obliterated. I guessed there wasn't much more I could do here. The wrecking crew soon started back to work, and I went back to my motel. I was in Washington by three o'clock that afternoon.

Four

Hawk's office was dark when I came in. He was at his desk, the movement on a small portable TV screen in front of him making shadows on his profile.

He didn't greet me. When I sat down across from him, he snapped on the desk light and shined it in my face. Then after surveying the damage for a moment or two, he snapped it off and went back to watching the set. "I hope you landed a few punches, anyway," he said gruffly.

"He wasn't like any man I've ever fought before," I said. "He was faster; his fists were as hard as that table top; and I swear he could see in the dark."

"This supposed to be some kind of excuse?"

"No, just fact."

He snapped on the light again and took another look at me. "I don't see anything that won't heal. How about the rest of you?"

"A broken rib, but I'm living with it."

He snapped the light off again. "I've been watching the news reports. This man Strommond is on the verge of becoming an international celebrity. They're even talking about the Nobel Prize."

"I don't think he did it," I said firmly.

"I agree with you. At least as far as to say there's something more going on here. The beating you took is proof of that. But it doesn't matter. It's not our problem any more."

"What do you mean?"

"I mean that everyone's satisfied that the defoliant is gone forever, with chances about a billion to one that it can ever be remade."

"But surely they know about what happened."

"A few do. They've left it up to me to take care of it, but we don't have the manpower to look into it ourselves. We just can't spare anybody."

"But, Sir, we can't just overlook this . . ."

"It'll be taken care of, but not directly. I called Hensen in Chicago last night. Told him there may be more to the Strommond story than they're telling. I even hinted I thought Strommond was lying. Hensen'll find out one way or the other. He's one of the best investigative reporters in the business."

He pulled a cigar out of his inside pocket and looked at me over his glasses as he lit it. "That doesn't satisfy you though, does it, Killmaster? You figure you've got a score to settle. Well, you may have to forego that pleasure for the time being. I've got another assignment for you, one that you're going to like. I'm sending you to the Riviera."

This was the last thing I wanted. I cleared my throat and chose my words with care. "You know I've never been one to refuse an assignment, Sir, but in view of the present state of my health, I'm going to have to respect-fully request some time off . . . ''

"So you can run back to Ann Arbor on your own? Forget it, Nick. Listen, I understand how you feel. If circumstances were different, I'd say sure, go on back and see what you can dig up. But the fact is I need you in the Riviera."

I let go a sigh. It galled me to leave something like this unfinished. But finally I said, "All right. What's the problem?"

Hawk switched off the TV and turned on the desk lamp. Then he pulled a file out of a lower desk drawer. "In the last week we've gotten two reports from John Mattingly, our operative in that part of the Mediterra-nean basin. Apparently, there's a yacht anchored in the harbor at Monaco belonging to a Swiss millionaire named Roman St. Germaine. Word has it there's enough bomb-making plutonium aboard that ship to double the U.S. arsenal. Already representatives from the Third World have landed in town. According to Mattingly, as soon as enough interested parties are present, the auction will start."

"And you want me to scuttle it."

"Right. Recover the plutonium intact. We'll dispose of it properly once you get it into this country."

"And you want me to just forget about Ann Arbor."

"For the time being. Nick, if I could give you time off to look into this business on your own, I'd do it. But this is urgent."

"All right," I said with a sign. "When do I leave?"

"Tonight. I've got you booked on the first plane. Use the cover name Andrew Caldwell. You're a nu-clear physicist and weapons expert vacationing in Europe. The ground work has already been laid.

Word's been spread that you're disenchanted with the
U.S. and are looking to sell your services to the highest
bidder. So be greedy. This Caldwell character likes to
live well, but he can't live on what he's paid here.''

''Then I get an expense account?''

''Within limits. There'll be credit cards so you can
make it look good, but don't go overboard.''

During the whole of the six-hour transatlantic flight I
stared out the window unable to sleep, reviewing every
detail of what had happened, looking for some sort of
clue to the reason why. Nothing seemed to fit.

At the Nice airport I rented the fastest car I could
find, a brand-new turbo-charged Porche Targa, and
took off along Le Grande Cornishe, the old highway
linking Nice and Monte Carlo that skirts the edges of
cliffs eight hundred feet above the Mediterranean. It
was a brilliant afternoon, the sun blazed in the sky, the
air was clear, and the wind whipped the ocean below
into flecks of white surf. I should have been exhila-
rated, high, but I wasn't. I had too much on my mind.

In Monte Carlo I had a reservation at the Loews, a big
new hotel right on the ocean with a gambling casino on
the main floor. It was an elegant place, really, designer
shops throughout the mezzanine, half a dozen restaurants and bars, a swimming pool on the roof. But
somehow it didn't matter to me—and for obvious
reasons.

The desk clerk gave me a broad smile when I handed
him my passport, then disappeared to check my name.
I took the opportunity to survey the lobby. It was
the height of the season, as they say, and the hotel
was overflowing. Everywhere I looked there were
scantily-clad bodies and white smiling teeth in brown
faces. A French girl, no more than twenty, but ele-

gantly dressed, turned from where she was perusing a shop window and gave me a curious stare. I smiled back.

The desk clerk returned, still smiling and dangling a key from a red plastic disc. "Four seventy-four in the new section," he said; then he rang a bell and a boy in a red jacket came forward to help me with my bag.

As I followed him along through the lobby, I realized I would have much preferred the Hotel de Paris just up the hill. It was smaller, older, more in the tradition of fine European hotels. In my present state of mind it would have suited me better than the free-wheeling holiday atmosphere of the Loews. But then it wouldn't have fit in with the Andy Caldwell cover, and that was the important thing.

Besides, the Loews had another advantage, which I discovered when I pulled open the drapes on the glass doors to the balcony off my room. There was a panorama of sea and sky and in the foreground an unobstructed view of the Monacan bay. From this vantage point I could see the comings and goings of every boat in the harbor.

I laid my suitcase on the bed and unpacked, then I showered, shaved, and dressed in a cashmere jacket suitable for an evening on the Riviera. When I was ready, my three weapons in their familiar places, I took the elevator to the lobby. Mattingly wasn't due for a while yet, and I wanted to find out what I could about St. Germaine as a kind of double-check of whatever he told me.

The crowd in the lobby seemed to be in the transition state between late afternoon and early evening. Many people were still in swimsuits, while others were dressed for dinner. The two restaurants and the discotheque, all of which were off the large main room, were full. Lines formed at the doors as people waited to get in. But it was still too early for action in the casino, so this is where I headed.

The room was virtually empty. Banks of slot machines stood silent along the outer wall, except for one kept busy by a young French couple, spending what was probably the last of their honeymoon cash. Croupiers and blackjack dealers lolled behind the tables, waiting for the after-dinner crowd.

It was dead except for a peculiar scene going on at the far end of the room. An area in front of a blackjack table had been cordoned off with velvet rope and around it had gathered a small group of onlookers. When I got closer, I saw what they were all staring at.

Hunched over the table, his back to the crowd, sat a well-dressed, compact little man furtively peeking under the corners of his cards. To one side was an enormous stack of ten thousand franc chips. The dealer was apparently waiting for him to decide whether he wanted another card, and from the look on the dealer's face, the game had been going on all afternoon.

Finally, the little man nodded. The dealer dealt face up. A four. The crowd stirred. It was his fourth card and they were sure he'd broken twenty-one and lost. But the man tapped the cards with his finger to indicate he was going to stand pat.

Then it was the dealer's turn. He rolled his cards face up. A queen and a five. Without hesitating he threw down another card. Another five. That made twenty.

The little man didn't seem in the least perturbed. He turned his hand over a card at a time. He had a four and a jack already showing. The next card was a three and the next . . . another four. The crowd stirred again and broke out in muted applause.

I'd been watching all this from the rear of the crowd

in a mirror that hung over the table, and what I saw was the reflection of the table top with the cards and hands of the players. As yet, I hadn't seen the face of the little gambler.

It wasn't until three security personnel showed up to help him carry his winnings over to the cashier's window that he finally turned around, but when he did I froze.

He was wearing a wig now to camouflage the scars on the side of his head, but those slitty little eyes were unmistakable. Here, halfway around the world, was the same man who'd beaten me to a near-pulp two days earlier!

In order to get through the crowd he had to pass right by me. I looked at him carefully to make sure I wasn't wrong. I wasn't. The wig didn't even fit right.

I stood only a few yards from the window while he cashed in, hating even the greedy little twitch about his mouth as the girl counted out his money. My first inclination was to wait for him outside and finish what we'd started back in Ann Arbor. But as I stood there plugging the slot machine and trying to look inconspicuous, it occurred to me that wouldn't be very smart.

As much as I wanted to pay him back for the pain he'd caused me, I had no idea if he even knew who I was. It was black as pitch in that basement. If I followed him, he might tell me more about who he was and who he was connected to than if I leaned on him—although I had to admit the prospect of leaning on him appealed to me. I don't mind taking a beating in the line of duty, but when there doesn't seem to be any reason for it, it does have a way of angering me.

The guards escorted him as far as the casino door. Then he slipped out into the crowded lobby, with me right behind him. He moved up the center of the room, across the strip of red carpeting that acted as a divider, and into the glut of people standing around the lobby bar.

I took care to act as nonchalantly as possible, my eyes darting here and there, trying to catch a glimpse of him. He was a hard man to tail because he was so small. He kept disappearing behind people and things, so I had to stay fairly close or lose him. Fortunately, he wore steel taps on his shoes. Out in the lobby the clicking sound gave him away, but here in the bar the carpet deadened my advantage.

There was some sort of uproar going on between the piano player and a group of drunken American tourists over a German song the piano player either didn't know or didn't want to play. It distracted me long enough to lose sight of him and I had to use a coralling technique to find him again. There was no door to the lobby bar and the room opened on one end into the main lobby area. I walked back and forth across this wide opening repeatedly until I spotted him out making his way out into the lobby again.

I caught up to him and for the next hundred yards we played cat and mouse. He stopped to gaze in the flower shop window; I bent down to pick a paper off the newsstand. He bought a pack of cigarettes; I was behind him in line waiting to pay for my paper. I couldn't tell if he knew I was following him or not. He seemed calm and unruffled, but sometimes that's a sure sign.

He stopped at the door of another shop and went in. It was a jewelry store having a sale in Italian gold. I started to follow him in, but then hesitated. The place was packed. I could easily lose him in the press of people, or worse yet, become separated by the dozens of shoppers between me and the door.

So instead I sat down on a convenient couch, opened

my paper, and resigned myself to wait. It was highly unlikely that there was any other than the one door, which meant sooner or later he'd have to come out the way he went in.

Ten minutes passed. Fifteen. I was beginning to wonder if he hadn't given me the slip.

A commotion erupted at the entrance to the hotel. I looked up and saw three large tour buses parked in the circular drive, each painted white, green, and red, the colors of the Italian flag. On the sidewalk in front of the buses stood a number of brawny young men, all carrying kit bags with the names of tennis shoe companies printed on them. Around the young men mobbed a multitude of newsmen and curiosity-seekers, mostly young women, so many in fact the huge open-air doors of the hotel were completely choked with people. It could only be the Italian soccer team in town for the tournament hosted every year by Prince Rainier's son. What had drawn my attention to all this activity was a shout that had gone up when two of the teammates had hoisted a third boy on their shoulders. Now they were parading him around the parking area, accompanied by more shouts of good fellowship and comraderie and squeals from the young women, all to the delight of the people from the press.

I was watching this, taking it all in, when I noticed a familiar compact figure making its way along the marble wall in front of the jewelry store. It was the Oriental, drawn to the noise like a rat to a piece of cheese, knowing this was just the diversion he needed to elude me.

I stood up. He was almost out of the hotel. He took the marble steps in quick, choppy strides and headed out the door just as the soccer team, newsmen, entourage, and all, headed in.

I was right behind him, up the steps, across the large door mats with the hotel insignia set into them. That was when I got caught in a tide of people. I kept pushing forward, and the flood kept pushing me back. I'd lost sight of him.

I grew frantic. The thought of him getting away was almost more than I could bear. I started pushing people from me, trying to swim above them so I could see.

Finally, I squeezed out the door, but he was gone. I looked around desperately. He'd disappeared. He wasn't on the sidewalk, nor was he in any of the cars parked nearby, and there hadn't been time for him to drive away.

That was a neat trick, I thought disgustedly. I turned and headed back into the lobby. Then I heard a familiar clicking sound on the concrete stairway to my right.

The stairwell ran down to the sea in front of the hotel. It was six steps, then a landing, then six more steps and another landing and on in that way for six or seven landings until it reached the road below. I came down these stairs as fast as I could, my feet barely touching each one, the clicking echoing on the concrete just ahead of me.

Two teenage boys didn't see me coming and had to press themselves against the wall to keep from being knocked down. One of them shouted after me as I hurried down.

I was getting closer now: I could hear him just one landing below me. I put on an extra burst of speed, rounded the last corner, and stopped short.

A middle-aged woman in a floppy Panama and sundress carrying a folding beach chair stared up at me in wide-eyed amazement. On her feet were a pair of high-heeled shoes.

"They're just old ones," she said with an English

accent, noticing my obvious interest in her footware. "I use them for knocking about."

I looked out over the stair railing in time to see a cab make the long curve from the front of the hotel and pull up at a stoplight before turning into the main road. The light changed and the cab sped by. In the backseat was the Oriental. He didn't bother to look up.

Five

I watched until the car disappeared around the harbor.

"Miss somebody, did you?" asked the woman. "Not to worry," she said, patting my hand as I gripped the railing. "She'll come back to the likes of you." Then she secured her beach chair serenely under her arm and began trudging up the stairs again.

I waited a minute, then followed her, stopping every few stairs to lean against the wall. My side felt like it was splitting open.

Finally, she came back down to have a closer look at me. "You all right?" she asked.

"Yes. I'm fine."

"Hurt yourself?" She looked down at my hand pressed against my rib cage.

"Long time ago. I shouldn't try to run."

"You don't look well. May I offer you an arm?"

"No, thank you. I can make it."

"You're sure?"

"Yes."

She took up her beach chair again and began her ascent. I followed, this time making a concerted effort not to look as though I were about to pass out.

I made it into the hotel, across the lobby, to the bank of elevators against one wall. My face was flushed I was sure, but other than that, I must have appeared fairly normal. Moving slowly, but normal nonetheless.

When the elevator came, it was empty. I got on and when the doors closed, I stood there staring down at the elevator carpeting. I began to turn the situation over in my mind. Something in all this was missing: some logical consequence of seeing that man twice in two days in localities ten thousand miles apart. But it hadn't hit me yet.

I got out on my floor and walked slowly down the hall. John Mattingly was knocking at the door to my room.

"Andy!" he called when he saw me. He came running, grinning like a Cheshire cat.

"John, it's good to see you," I said. He pumped my hand like a Shriner at a convention. It was an act. Part of the reason Hawk had chosen the Caldwell cover for me was the fact that Caldwell and Mattingly had attended M.I.T. together and had been brothers in the same fraternity. This way a legitimate relationship had already been established, so there was no need for us to slip around trying to meet in secret. It was meant as a convenience, but I wasn't holding up my end of the charade very well.

When he came close, Mattingly leaned over and said in a low whisper, "You look like hell."

"I'm okay. I just need to sit down."

He helped me to the door and I fumbled for the key,

opened the door, and let us in. Unable to stand by this time, I opted for the bed. "I got banged up a couple of days ago," I told him. "I would've been all right, if I hadn't tried to run a four-minute mile just now."

"A four-minute mile? Whatever for?"

"I'll tell you later. There's a strip of elastic bandage in my case," I said, motioning toward the closet. "Get it for me."

He went over and opened my suitcase while I undid the bandage I'd put on in Washington. When he came back, my side was uncovered.

"Jesus! That's a bruise," he said. "That must hurt like hell. Have you seen a doctor?"

"There's nothing a doctor can do. Let me have that." I took the wad of bandage from him and put it next to me on the bed. Then I gingerly undid Wilhelmina's holster and laid it on the nightstand. Next I took the bandage and began unrolling it around my middle.

"I can't believe they'd send you on an assignment in your condition. What's Hawk thinking anyway?"

"He thinks I can take care of myself. Here, help me with this."

Mattingly took the bandage and began unraveling it, pussy-footing around the big splotch of black and yellow under my arm.

"No, tighter. Cinch me up good and tight."

Mattingly pulled on the bandage and the pain made me wince.

"Don't stop," I told him.

"You won't be able to breathe."

"Let me worry about breathing. Just make it tight as you can."

He pulled again and the flesh around the elastic turned white. He made several laps around my chest, then pinned it. "I think you're crazy."

"Just give me my shirt." I put it on and leaned back against the head of the bed. Then I lit a cigarette and for several minutes neither of us said anything while I smoked.

Finally, I stuffed the butt in the bottom of the ashtray. "So," I said.

"So?"

"So tell me about St. Germaine."

"St. Who?"

"St. Germaine, the man whose ship is carrying the stuff."

"What stuff? What are you talking about?"

"You mean you don't know?"

"Am I supposed to? I just assumed *you* were going to brief *me*."

"And you haven't the foggiest idea what I'm talking about."

He shrugged.

I should have known. Here was the logical consequence I couldn't put my finger on in the elevator. Two appearances by my little friend, two assignments fizzled. I was being set up again, like a sucker on the wrong end of a one-two combination.

"So obviously somebody screwed up," Mattingly was saying. "They forgot to send me my end of it. That doesn't mean I don't want to be part of it. I'm ready for a little action. You wouldn't believe how boring this place can be at times."

"You don't understand, John. I'm here because of reports you sent in."

"Reports? I didn't send in any reports."

"I know. That's the problem."

"Somebody must have forged them."

"That's not possible. They came in verbally by scrambler."

He shook his head and I could see he was genuinely stumped.

"About a week ago, we received a communication with your voice print stating that an influx of technical people were coming here from various Arab countries, principally Jordan and Syria. You speculated it might be some kind of secret summit, a sharing of technologies between the two countries.

"Two days later another report, also in your voice, stated that rumors you'd heard led you to suspect that an auction was going to be conducted in secret, in which high-grade plutonium cores would be offered for sale. You said you would seek to confirm.

"Three days passed and we heard nothing from you. Then in comes this last report in which you said an underwater search of the harbor had revealed a high reading of radioactivity aboard a ship owned by a Swiss millionaire named Roman St. Germaine. You said chances were good this was where the plutonium was being kept, but you would wait for help before investigating further."

"These reports you're talking about are complete fabrications," Mattingly said firmly. "I never sent them."

"Somebody did."

"It wasn't me."

"John, we both know it's virtually impossible to forge one of these reports. Your voice print is as distinctive as your thumb print. There's no way someone could duplicate it."

"Nonetheless, someone did, because I'm telling you, I never sent in any such reports. I don't know anything about any plutonium and I never heard of Romaine St. Germaine, or whatever his name is."

"No need to get yourself worked up," I said. "I

believe you. Here.'' I took a cigarette out of the pack on the bed, then threw the pack to him. He caught it and took one out. I watched as he lit it. His hands were steady; he seemed calm, but resolute. Either he was a better agent than I'd been led to believe, or he wasn't in on setting me up. ''So tell me,'' I said, after the smoke had cleared somewhat, ''how's it possible to forge a report?''

''Maybe bits of tape all spliced together?''

I shook my head. ''No, that's the very thing the voice analyzer on the Washington end is designed to pick up. I don't think it can be done with a tape. And I don't think it's possible for someone to imitate your voice, either, no matter how good he is.''

''How then?''

''I can think of one way, although it's not very likely. One might be able to reproduce your speech apparatus bionically and program in your speech pattern.''

''That's outrageous. No one can do that.''

''Not without extensive X-rays of your mouth and larynx.'' Mattingly's expression suddenly changed. ''What's the matter?''

''I had root canal work done about a month ago. They took X-rays then.''

''Of your throat, too?''

''Yes. I asked them at the time if all the X-rays were really necessary and they asured me they were. They said the doctor liked to be thorough and there was no extra charge.''

''I'll bet there wasn't. And you weren't the least bit suspicious?''

''Not at the time. I had no reason . . . '' He didn't finish whatever he was going to say. For several minutes we sat in silence, I on the bed and Mattingly in an armchair across from me. The sun had set and the red sky tinted the room a dim pink. I couldn't see much of his face anymore, just the red tip of his cigarette, glowing brightly now and then in the darkness.

Finally, he asked, "Where does that leave us? Shouldn't we be doing something? Rushing to tell someone?"

"This isn't the first time this has happened," I said candidly, "my being sent on a wild goose chase. Earlier this week I had an assignment in Ann Arbor, Michigan, and it turned out to be a mirage just like this one. Only somebody engineered it. I was set up. I followed a lead, a simple, inevitable lead from the information I'd been given, and walked headlong into a trap. Now it's happening again. This time I'm going to be more careful. But I don't want anyone interfering with it until I find out who's doing this to me and why."

Mattingly cleared his throat significantly. "Excuse me, old boy," he said, "but isn't that a trifle egocentric of you? I mean if I understand all this correctly, duplicating my voice is only part of it. In order to file a false report, one would also have to break the code by which the scrambler transmits my voice. Isn't that true?"

"Right."

"Which means if they know the code well enough to put data in, they can probably get data out."

"Most likely."

"And if that's true, then the potential exposure of sensitive information is incredible. Weapons systems, troop strengths, missile emplacements, the whereabouts of every nuclear submarine—it staggers the imagination. In other words, the entire balance of world power is in danger, and you think all this has been accomplished merely to lead you into a trap? I hate to say it, old man, but that doesn't sound altogether reasonable."

"Maybe not, but you're forgetting something."

"What's that?"

"The key to a code is valuable only so long as no one knows you have it. Otherwise, the code is changed and you're right back where you started. Now, in this situation, no one has made any attempt to disguise the fact of the matter. As soon as you and I got together and compared notes, the truth became obvious. Therefore, there must be more going on here than mere code-breaking. Somebody's up to something even bigger, or they wouldn't be so unconcerned about letting everybody know."

" 'Everybody' meaning you and me, because as far as you're concerned, we're not going to tell anybody else."

I nodded. "Not for the time being, anyway."

"All right, I'll go along with this," he sighed, "up to a point. But if you don't get some results pretty fast, I'm going to have to let the home office in on it."

"Agreed." I put my cigarette out carefully in the ashtray. He bent over and snuffed his cigarette too, and dropped the butt in next to mine. The room by now was completely dark. The only light came from the reflection in the open balcony doors.

"Meanwhile," Mattingly went on after a minute, breaking the tension, "I'm at your disposal. Where shall we start?"

"Roman St. Germaine. Is there any way you can find out which boat down there, if any, is his?"

"Nothing could be simpler. That's what I do around here. I'm the harbor engineer."

"Good. Then you'll probably have access to a wet suit and diving gear."

"As a matter of fact, I can get you completely outfitted in about fifteen minutes."

"Do it. And I'll meet you under the bridge in front of the hotel."

He got up to go. Then he stopped at the door and turned around. He started to say something, then didn't, and opened the door and left.

Once he was gone, I got up slowly from the bed and walked to the balcony. Down below, the harbor lights shimmered on the water. Maybe Mattingly was right, I thought. If not codes, then what? How big could this thing be?

Six

I was under the bridge staring out at the darkening sea when I saw Mattingly's silhouette come loping down over the large rocks in my direction, dragging a sea bag behind him.

"I got everything you'll need," he said, swinging the bag so it came to rest at my feet. He opened it and began pulling things out and setting them on the rocks.

"Did you get a Geiger counter?" I asked hopefully.

He shook his head. He pulled out several more pieces of equipment, flippers, mask, snorkel, small water-proof flashlight. I crouched down beside him and began looking the stuff over.

"What about tanks?"

"No tanks. I figured without a Geiger counter there isn't much sense making an inspection of the hull. Besides, tanks are complicated. That means I've got to start the compressor and that means noise."

"So I guess I'm boarding the ship."

"I guess so." He took a length of nylon line with a grappling hook at one end out of the sack and handed it to me. "For boarding," he said.

I tossed it up and down in my hand a couple of times,

getting the feel of it. It was big, but lightweight enough
to throw and swim with. "This is going to have to be
padded," I said.

"Way ahead of you." He pulled two argyle socks
out of his pocket and fitted them over the tines of the
hook. Then out of his other pocket he produced two
short strands of wire and proceeded to fasten the socks
securely. "I had to make do in a hurry," he said.

"You did a good job," I said, happy with the outfitting he'd done. I sat down on a rock and took off my
shoes, socks and shirt. Then I stood and unzipped by
trousers. Underneath I had on a brief nylon swimming
suit. Mattingly watched all this sober-faced.

"What's the problem?" I asked.

"Your bandage."

"I can swim with it. Don't worry. I'll be all right.
The freedom of movement in the water will do me
good."

He nodded, but the look of concern didn't leave his
face.

"You think I'm walking into another trap."

"This is the most logical, inevitable lead, isn't it?
Isn't that where you'd lay a trap?"

"I suppose." The last two things he'd pulled out of
the bag were the two pieces of a wet suit. I coated the
inside of the bottoms of these with some talcum powder
he'd also brought and began to struggle my way into
them.

"There are only two of us who know about the
information leak in the AXE system. If anything hap-
pens to you."

"I'll be careful." I stood up and powdered the inside
of the rubber jacket, then gingerly put it on and zipped
it.

He came over to straighten the tails. "How's the elastic?" he asked, giving my ribs a pat.

"Fine. Nice and tight. The wet suit'll keep it dry."

He looked me over and nodded. "Then I guess I better tell you something about this boat. She's a big one, a hundred feet or more. In a yacht that size the crew sleeps forward, the owner aft. The engines are amidship and if she's hauling anything as heavy as the lead shielding needed to handle that much plutonium, she'd have to carry it under the engines or you'd notice it. She's in the fourth slip, second pier. Her name's *Astoria*."

"So he's definitely here."

"Been in port about a week."

I stooped down and fitted my feet into the flippers.

"Good luck," he said.

I thanked him and jumped from a rock feet first into the water. When I surfaced, I saw him watching me, his form a dim outline in the reflected light of the street lamps of the road above. "I'll be waiting in your room," he called after me.

I turned and began swimming. The water was sleek and black and I fell into a mechanical stroke that put a fair amount of distance quickly between me and the shore. For the first half of the swim the tide was weak and I cut through the water easily. Then I came around the point in front of the hotel and the surf picked up. About this time my ribs began to ache and I was reduced to a side-stroke.

Luckily, the harbor wasn't far. When I made my way between the breakwaters, the surface of the water flattened out, and sounds came to me from the city: traffic noises, then voices and music, and the clinking of ice in glasses.

I swam up the row of bobbing hulls between the second and third piers, stroking as silently as I could through the slicks of diesel oil and gasoline. I counted the slips. Fourth from the end and there she was, a gleaming white pleasure boat that, from the waterline, looked to be about the size of the Queen Mary. The name *Astoria* was printed in gold letters under the pilot house.

I swam gingerly until I was below the bow. All the activity seemed to be confined to the rear. The lights were on in the aft cabins, and in the large windows I could see figures moving.

I took the coil of thin nylon line off its hook on my suit and unwound it. Then I attached the grappling hook to one end and threw the hook the fifteen feet or so up to the forward bulwark. It landed with a soggy thud and caught under the railing. I tested it. It felt secure, so I started to climb. I pulled myself up hand over hand, knowing this was going to be the worst part of it. I kicked my flippers off and gripped with my feet, every time I inched up. but a dull pain shot through my side.

Finally, I pulled myself over the railing and slipped down onto the deck. There was no one in sight. For a moment I just lay there, breathing heavily and holding my rib cage; then I picked myself up and scurried in a low crouch for the anchor housing. From there I could see into the pilot house, where the light was off and it looked deserted.

I waited a few seconds, then stood up and crept silently down the gangway on the starboard side of the pilot house, looking for the stairwell that led to the crew's quarters, hoping to gain access from there to the engine room.

I found the stairs on the far side of the gangway (by practically stumbling into them in the dark) and began to climb down, listening to every movement. There was some sort of entertainment going on in the aft section. I could hear voices, mostly male.

At the bottom of the stairs was a short gangway with two of the crew's bunks on either side. At the end of it, a hatch, which I opened, led to another gangway with two more bunks and a common bath.

Another hatch led me into the galley. Everything here was scrubbed and battened down, the counter surfaces all gleaming in the florescent light that had been left on over the stove. As I stood there for a minute, with the feeling something had changed. It didn't hit me for several seconds, then I realized that I wasn't hearing the voices any more.

I pushed the swinging door into the dark next room, which was the dining area. I stepped in carefully, but I hadn't any more than cleared the doorway when something hit me in the back of the head and I went down.

Although the blow stunned me, it didn't knock me out. I lay on the floor in a state of limbo, a foot planted firmly in either of two worlds, one of dreams, the other reality. I was still conscious, but I couldn't move.

A light went on and there was a scuffling of shoes and voices. Two, three, I couldn't count them. Then somebody said, "Sit him in the chair," and two pairs of hands grabbed me and hoisted me to my feet. I was dazed, shaking my head to throw off the stupor, when the hands grabbed me again and shoved me into a chair.

"Let him come around," said another voice with a heavy French accent, which I gradually came to realize belonged to the stocky, red-haired man with the heavily lined face sitting in front of me. "Who are you?" he asked.

"Andy Caldwell."

"What are you doing aboard this ship?"

"Just looking it over. I'm thinking of buying one."

He cracked me a good one with his open hand along the side of my face. "Don't be wise with me, Monsieur. It is not healthy. I ask you again. What are you doing aboard this ship?"

"Some friends told me you had something for sale. I was just checking. I wanted to see it for myself."

"What friends, Monsieur? What did they tell you?"

"They told me you have something on board that's so hot not everyone knows how to handle it. I thought maybe I could help. I know something about these things."

"What things? Ach," he said disgustedly, "I don't know what you are saying."

"He's lying," said one man, stepping forward. "He knows."

"The hell he does," argued another.

The red-haired man held up his hand to quiet everybody. "It matters nothing whether he knows or not. Take him below. We'll head out to sea and dump him."

The two meaty ones on either side each grabbed an arm before I could do anything about it. I struggled for a minute, but it was hopeless. With two arms for one of mine, they were more than a match for me.

"Search him," the red-haired man said.

The two gripped me tighter and a third man stepped up and unzipped the jacket of my wet suit. He looked like a typical member of French low-life, the kind one finds hanging around waterfront bars in seaports like Marseilles and Le Havre, men who've sunk about as low as they can, and really have no compunction about slitting a throat for small change.

"*Qu'est que c'est?*" snorted Low-life when he discovered my bandage. "Has somebody winged my little chicken?" He slapped it roughly and a bolt of pain made me wince. "Does it hurt, chicken?" He jabbed it again. I spat in his face.

"*Sacre bleu!*" he roared, and reared back with a punch designed to take my head off. But the red-haired man caught his arm.

"Jacques!" he shouted. "Later you can have him for a little fun, no? Right now we search him and be done with it."

Low-life looked at the red-haired man with obvious distaste, then turned to me and glowered. But he did what he was told. He pulled off my jacket and found Hugo, my stiletto, strapped to my arm. The discovery made him grunt with satisfaction.

"The chicken has teeth," he said.

Then he pulled down the bottoms. It was everything I could do to keep from kneeing him in the face when he pushed the wetsuit down around my ankles, but I'd already decided on a plan that was going to require all my strength.

The two holding my arms lifted me off the floor so their friend could finish stripping the bottoms off. "*Rien,*" he told the red-haired man, and the red-haired man motioned with a jerk of his head for the others to take me out.

They moved me toward the door, which was much too narrow to allow us to pass three abreast. They had to turn me, one of the men going through ahead of me and one behind. I waited until I was a little more than halfway through, then made my move.

With a strong jerk of my arm I broke the grip of the man behind me. Then I flung the first man forward and pushed the door shut after us. It was the old idea of divide and conquer. The second man, the red-haired man, Low-life, and the rest of them were all contained back in the room, while the first man and I battled it out in the narrow passage way on the other side of the door.

The trick now was to take care of the one, while holding the door on the others. I managed to switch positions with him in the cramped space and use his back as a doorstop while I pounded on him for all I was worth. I'd caught him by surprise and I wasn't going to give him a chance to recover. I wanted to knock him cold and leave his big frame lying there so the others would have to push it out of the way.

I peppered him as hard as I could, but he wouldn't go down. He crouched against the door, taking my blows in the back and shoulders, but no place vulnerable. Time was running out. In a few seconds they were going to force the door. Finally, I kicked him in the kidneys. That straightened him up long enough for me to clip him on the jaw. He still wasn't out, but was dazed enough, and the others had already managed to push the door open a few inches. It was time to make a run for it.

I took off down the passageway with no idea of where I was going. At the end I found a short spiral staircase and charged up it. Behind me the door had opened and I could hear footsteps in pursuit.

At the top of the stairs was the main salon, about the size of a large living room, with glass windows on three sides looking out over the harbor. There was a door in the far wall and I raced for it, but half-way across a shot rang out that kicked up stuffing in the lounge chair just in front of me. I stopped short and turned to see where it had come from.

Two men were sitting casually in large armchairs. One wore a yachting cap and a blue blazer. Stuck in his eye was a monocle and beneath his nose hung a Kaiser Wilhelm mustache. This, I gathered, was Roman St.

Germaine. Next to him sat a small dark man with a smoking .32 in his hand.

"*Halten Sie!*" St. Germaine said, then added in English, "or the next one won't miss."

I looked at the door on the other side of the room, a good twenty-five feet away. He could squeeze off one, maybe two, shots before I could get there. Then I had to gamble it wasn't locked and pull it open

While I was figuring all this, the men from downstairs poured up the steps and into the salon. In the lead was Low-life. Without a moment's hesitation, he rushed up to me and hit me as hard as he could in the ribs. I folded up like a Christmas drunk.

As I lay on the floor squirming in pain, they stood around me in a circle and stared. They were talking, but I didn't catch much of what they said.

Then they pulled me erect, tied my hands and feet, and dragged me back down the passageway I'd just come up. They opened the door of the fiddley and took me in. Here was the engine room I'd been trying to locate. Two mammoth diesel engines were mounted side by side on steel cross bars. Between them was a trap door. The red-haired man opened the trap and Low-life and another man threw me in. Then they replaced the door and I could hear something heavy being dragged over it.

Seven

I lay in the darkness for several minutes, shaking from the pain welling up in waves from my side. Above me the two big diesel engines roared into action, and I knew there wasn't going to be much time. They wanted to kill me, but they wanted to do their dirty work someplace safely removed from Monte Carlo.

I began worming my way along the bottom of the hold, looking for something, anything sharp enough to cut the rope they'd used to tie me. But movement, I found, wasn't easy. With my feet bound and my hands trussed up behind my back, about all I could do was push myself along on my one shoulder and the side of my face while a couple of inches of bilge water sloshed over me every time the boat took a wave.

I made enough progress, though, to find a broad shelf, set about six inches off the bottom that extended across the breadth of the hull. I pulled myself up and rolled onto it. It was a relief to be out of the fetid stench of the bilge, but much hotter. The engines above were

just warming up and already the air was searing and
thick with diesel exhaust.

I inched my way around and found casks, boxes, and
crates on the shelf, the stores of the engine room. In one
crate was a spare manifold cover with its edges exposed. I rolled over, sat up (which put my head flush
against the hot engine decking), and maneuvered myself backward until I felt the sharp edge of metal with
my hands. Then I sawed furiously.

I kept it up for two minutes, maybe three, before I
slumped down on my side to take a rest. I felt the rope
with my fingers. The fibers hadn't been cut.

I gave up on the manifold cover and started moving
again, still looking. The next several crates were sealed
tight against water damage and had no metal on them
ragged enough to do the job. But beyond these and to
the rear there'd been a little shipboard accident. A large
crate of engine parts had fallen on another crate and
split it open. I wasn't sure what the second crate contained. Some kind of shoes. They smelled like horse
manure and had an eely feel. But the banding used to
close the box had burst on impact and a large coil of it
was laying out on the floor.

I rolled onto my back and picked the banding up
between my fingers, holding it edge-wise. Then I
pressed the knot against it between the small of my back
and an adjacent crate, and worked it up and down until
the banding came through and started to chafe my skin.
Then I pulled apart the few strands that remained and
untied my feet.

I was free, but I still needed a weapon. I began
rummaging in the dark through the boxes and crates
nearest to me. I found a set of wrenches, but they
wouldn't be much good unless I wanted to throw them.
There were cage lights with drop cords, cans of some

kind of paint, various tools, a keg of assorted nuts and bolts, but no weapon, nothing I could use against a knife or gun.

I was about to give up, thinking that even if there were one to be found, I'd never locate it in the dark; but then I got lucky. In the back, behind a stack of six or seven cases of what felt like motor oil I found an ancient tin box, covered with bilge debris. I crawled back to the other crates with it and opened it with the help of one of the wrenches. Inside was a flare gun with two flares; one of them had propellant crystalized on its casing, but the other looked usable.

I held the empty pistol in my hand to get the feel of it, then loaded the good flare in behind the barrel. On my hands and elbows I crawled to the end of the shelf and let myself down. Then I made my way in a crouch to the thin line of light coming through the trap door of the engine room.

I hadn't gone more than a step or two when I encountered a number of foul-smelling slippers floating in the bilge water. I had no idea what they were or what they were doing in the engine room supplies.

It was definitely a slipper rather than a shoe, and from the feel of it, the uppers were beaded in a Turkish design like those I'd seen for sale to tourists in a bazaar at Ankara.

Turkish. I turned that idea over and my suspicion began to grow. I took the slipper, scrambled back onto the shelf, and crawled to where the crate had burst open.

It was a big crate, close to a thousand pairs of slippers, I estimated. And as I examined them, I noticed something that they were all the same size.

I found the end of the banding and used it to cut the seam stitching of the upper sole. Nothing. I cut open the lower, which was made of soft, padded leather. Inside was a tin foil packet of powder. I touched a fingertip of it to my tongue. Heroin, very pure and, from the lumps in it, in a very raw state. So this was St. Germaine's game. Not plutonium at all, but drug smuggling.

I threw the slipper back in with the others and made my way with the flare gun back to the trap door. I'd heard them weight it down with something heavy when they'd closed it. Now I could only hope whatever that something was, it wasn't so big it couldn't be dislodged a little. I lay face up in the bottom, with my back on the center beam and both feet planted on the trap door. Then I began to buck with everything I had.

The door moved slightly. Whatever was on top gave way a bit, then fell back with a jolt. I tried it again. Then again.

I didn't really think I could move it, but I knew someone would be on duty up above to keep an eye on me. They wouldn't leave me unattended. And I thought my chances were good that the guard would be my old friend, Low-life. He'd jump at the opportunity to do more damage to me, and I felt sure when the assignment was passed out, he took it. And if it was him up there and he saw me bouncing whatever it was up and down, he'd open the door himself like a fool, instead of running for help.

I heard some activity on the metal floor above me, even over the enormous din of the engines. I kicked all the harder. I heard scraping. The object over the door was being dragged aside.

"Don't fret, chicken," Low-life snickered, "I'm coming."

I gripped the flare gun resting on my chest and pulled back the hammer, aiming right about where his head would be when he opened the door.

He fumbled with the metal ring on the door then pulled it open. I fired.

The flare caught him full in the mouth, gagging him. He fell back trying to pull it out, but he couldn't. The propellant forced it in, lodging it in his throat. As I watched from the trap door, he writhed back and forth on the deck vomiting flame.

Then the propellant ran out and for an awful second there was nothing. He redoubled his effort to get the cardboard tubing out of his mouth, but it was jammed in too far. The more he tried, the more of it he swallowed. Finally, he realized it was hopeless and he looked over at me, his hands shaking. Then the main charge went off and his face exploded in a burst of light.

I hoisted myself from my make-shift prison and dashed across the floor of the engine room. There wasn't much time. Low-life lay against one wall, his face a blackened hole, a tongue of phosphorescent flame still spurting from his mouth.

I grabbed a fire axe off the wall and broke the main fuel line in the left-hand engine. Diesel oil began pumping over the engine and onto the floor in rivulets to where Low-life was lying. In a few seconds, a blaze erupted and billows of black smoke filled the room.

I moved toward the door, keeping low where the air was reasonably breathable. It wouldn't take long for the fire to set off the alarm up on the bridge, and I wanted to be in position when they broke down the door to get to it.

Flames licked the walls. Both engines suddenly stopped. They'd cut off the ignitions from above. The diesel fuel would stop pumping, but it didn't matter. The fire was big enough to burn the bulkhead and the wood decking.

The lights suddenly went out. Except for the fire the

room was dark. I reached up and secured the latch on the door, effectively locking myself in. If they didn't come down and force an entry in the next two minutes, I would die in the inferno alongside Low-life.

I waited. Then I heard them outside shouting at one another in French. They rattled the knob, then threw their shoulders against the door. I crouched to one side. They rammed the door again. This time the wood around the latch strained but didn't give way. More shouting, then after what seemed an intolerably long time, someone fetched an axe. They chopped until there was a hole in the door large enough to poke an arm through. Another few seconds, and the door sprung open.

They came piling in, several confused silhouettes, batting at the smoke with their hands.

"Pierre, run tell the captain. Jacques? Where's Jacques?"

I stood up, my back to the wall beside the door, holding my breath. When I thought they were all in, I slipped around the jamb of the door and took off running.

I'd miscalculated by one Frenchman. As I came careening down the passageway, a big brute of a man rounded the partition just in front of me. He walked right into a left hand that had all the force in my arm plus all the weight of my moving body behind it. It caught him square in the Adam's apple, and he went down choking.

I was running down the same passage again, just as I had earlier, only this time I knew exactly where I was going. On the upper deck, behind the pilot house there was a small launch I'd seen when I'd swum out to the boat. I had to make it at least that far.

The ship was in mortal danger, that much I knew.

Although the fuel tanks themselves wouldn't explode unless the fire in the engine room got a good deal hotter, the engine room was only a short distance from the galley, and the stoves in the galley would have to operate on propane gas. Once the fire got to those tanks, she'd explode.

As I ran up the stairs to the main salon, I heard the siren for general alarm begin to whine. Very soon they'd realize the direness of the situation and the bell to abandon ship would sound. At that point the launch would become the most valuable piece of equipment on board.

I raced across the room, St. Germaine and his little gun-toting friend no longer anywhere in sight. I made it through the door to the deck on the other side, then grabbed the edge of the upper deck, that formed a roof for the salon, and pulled myself up.

I was in luck. The launch was still where I'd seen her, covered with a tarp. I rushed over, unfastened the tarp, and flung it into the dark sea. Then I turned the little boat around nose-first and was about to push it in the water when St. Germaine popped out of the pilot house door.

He saw what I was up to, but was too far away to do anything about it. Then it must have dawned on him all at once, the urgent condition of his vessel and the fact that I was taking the only means of escape, leaving him to either swim for it or go down with the ship. It occurred to me, as I looked at him, that perhaps he didn't know about the heroin, or that he'd never really given himself up to the role of a drug smuggler if he did. He was still a yachtsman, temporarily tolerating the presence of some undesirables on board, for the sake of money.

It was a strange confrontation. We must have stood

looking at one another for a full twenty seconds without moving. Then an explosion below caused the ship to lurch, jolting both of us back to reality and the business at hand.

I pushed the launch off into the blackness of space and waited for the splash as she hit the water. Then I jumped after it. Above me somewhere St. Germaine was yelling something unintelligible in German.

I swam up to the boat and pulled myself on board. Then I pull-started the tiny outboard on the back. She revved to life on the first try and in a few minutes I was skimming across the crests of the waves in the direction I hoped was shore.

I hadn't gone more than a quarter mile when the *Astoria* exploded. The force of the blast lifted her several feet out of the water and split her hull in two. She must have sunk very quickly—the last of the visible fires was out in a matter of minutes.

Eight

I set the outboard for half-throttle, then lay back against the stern for a rest. It was a beautiful night, temperate and clear. I spotted the North Star and used it to set my course, knowing that as long as I headed in a northerly direction, I'd hit land.

In a few minutes I was sound asleep. When I awoke, I was out of gas and the boat was drifting south. I had no idea how long I'd been out or how far I'd traveled in the wrong direction.

What was more, the sea was becoming rougher. My small boat was being tossed up and down like flotsam. I found a pair of oars lacquered white to match the boat. They weren't intended as much more than ornamentation, but there were locks for them and I laid to.

I rowed for an hour or more, always with the North Star to my back, then my side began giving me trouble. I stayed with it another half hour, then quit. I was played out. If I didn't get some sleep soon, I'd collapse and wouldn't have to worry about making it to shore at all.

I wrapped myself in one of the two life jackets and curled up in the bow, using the other as a pillow. The sea rolled and the little boat rose and fell with each wave. I did my best to forget where I was and let sleep, that ancient healer, overtake me.

When I woke up for the second time, the sun was high overhead. At first all I saw was the expanse of the blue sea. But when I turned my head, I saw the cliffs of Monte Carlo all pink in the afternoon sun. It was a welcome sight.

I decided to swim the rest of the way to the beach inlet that led up to the hotel. I jumped into the warm water and left the launch to drift out to sea. When I reached shore and stood up for the first time, I realized how shaky I was—that my ordeal of the past few days was taking its toll. I stood there a few minutes trying to restore my balance and decided the best place for me would be my hotel room.

I climbed the rocks, then walked up the stairs and into the lobby. No one thought anything of me. I was just another swimmer among hundreds of swimmers. Up in my room Mattingly was waiting with some interesting news.

When I entered my room I found one of the easy chairs in front of the double glass doors and Mattingly sound asleep in it. His unshaven face was turned to one side, his mouth gaping, a pair of binoculars resting on his chest.

I nudged him on the shoulder and he sat bolt upright and stared at me.

"Nick! Where the hell have you been?"

"All in good time, pal." I wondered if I looked as bad as I felt. Mattingly answered that question for me.

"You don't look too good. You'd better sit down."
He pulled the second easy chair up next to his. I sat
down and let my body go. I could have fallen asleep on
the spot.

"I'll call room service and have them send us up a
drink."

"Good idea."

He went to the phone as I stared out at the sunlight
dancing on the waves breaking against the barriers of
the far side of the harbor. In a minute he was back.

"So let's have it."

I gave him a blow-by-blow run down of everything
that happened. He listened carefully, interrupting only
when the drinks arrived. After that he sat in his chair
and nodded while he sipped his gin and tonic. He didn't
stop me again until I got to the heroin in the ship's hull.

"Then there wasn't any plutonium on board after
all."

"No."

"And it was another set-up."

I nodded and took another drink from my glass. The
alcohol was beginning to do its job. I was coming
undone slowly, a bit at a time, like an overwound
spring.

"Why did they think you were there?" asked Mattingly.

"I'm not really sure. It wasn't plutonium. I mentioned that and drew a blank. Someone must've told
them I was a narc. They knew I was coming. They were
waiting for me on the other side of that galley door."

"So you don't think they were in on the set-up?"

"No. My bet is that someone told them a story." I
took another long drink from my glass, nearly draining
it. "I sure as hell would like to find out who."

"As a matter of fact, you might not have long to

wait. There was a woman here last night looking for Nick Carter. Said she had a message for him.''

''What did you tell her?''

''What could I tell her? I told her I never heard of him.''

''What did she look like?''

''Small. Long black hair, very pretty. Japanese, I think.''

''She leave a name or an address?''

He shook his head. ''We haven't seen the last of her, though.''

''What do you mean by that?''

He went and got a fur stole that was hanging in the closet and tossed it in my lap. ''She left this.''

It was silver fox with a designer's tag in it. Worth two thousand, maybe more. But there was no name, nothing to identify it.

''This is an expensive calling card,'' I said. ''Did she look like she could afford to leave something like this behind?''

''Hard to say. This is the Riviera, remember. Here stoles like that are commonplace. She was well-dressed, though.''

''Still, a woman doesn't just come with a wrap and not leave with it. Not unless she's very upset.''

''She was. When I told her I'd never heard of Nick Carter, she got very insistent. Told me to drop all the cloak and dagger stuff and talk to her straight.''

''And what did you say?''

''I told her I didn't know what she was talking about. She invited herself in and took off the wrap. We talked for a few minutes, then all of a sudden she just got up and walked out. Nervous as a cat the whole time she was here.''

I turned the stole over in my hand, trying to think.

"Obviously she knows something. Only three people are aware I'm here. You, Hawk, and the guy who's engineered this wild goose chase."

"And she doesn't get her information from me or from Hawk."

"Exactly." It was a beautiful garment. The skins of fox fur had been masterfully selected and carefully stitched together. "I know a girl who fits the description," I said, "but with her it's more likely a sweatsuit than designer furs."

"Never predict what a woman will wear," Mattingly said philosophically. "It doesn't matter. She'll be back. Mark my words." He finished his drink and put the empty glass down on the coffee table. "What's on the agenda now?"

"R and R, at least for the next few hours," I said, laying the stole on the arm of the chair and standing up. "I'm exhausted. I need a shower and some sleep. Come back later and we'll hit the casinos. I'm going to find that gambler if I have to turn this town inside out."

Mattingly stood up, too. "All right," he said, "I'll be back around ten."

Once he was gone, I peeled off the bathing suit and slipped into the shower. I took my time, savoring the hot water as it cascaded over me. When I came out, I was so tired, all I could think of was sleep. I put Wilhelmina under the pillow and fell on the bed without bothering to turn the covers down. I was out before the man could say ten.

Nine

I don't remember what woke me, some movement or sound, perhaps nothing more than a premonition that I wasn't alone in the room. At any rate, as if by instinct, my eyes shot open and my body, while still relaxed, became alert, ready to spring if the need arose.

I examined my field of vision without turning my head. Nothing. Then a silhouette moved stealthily across the oblong of light created by the balcony doors. My hand gripped Wilhelmina where she lay hidden under the pillow.

Something made of paper was placed on the coffee table. Then the silhouette recrossed the doors on its way to the exit.

I rolled over and turned on the light. ''Hello, Gigi,'' I said.

Gigi Minamoto stared at me from the other side of the room. ''I thought you were asleep.''

I got off the bed and pulled my bathrobe on, keeping Wilhelmina trained on her. ''Why? What have we got to hide from one another?''

I squinted at her while my eyes adjusted to the light. She'd changed since I'd seen her in Phoenix. There were worry-lines around her mouth I hadn't seen before.

She eyed Wilhelmina warily. "Is that really necessary?" she said, indicating the gun.

"I don't know. A man in my position can't be too careful. Sit down."

She placed herself in one of the easy chairs and crossed her legs. She was trying to look composed, she wasn't fooling me. Underneath that exterior she was afraid of something.

"How'd you get in?" I asked.

"I bribed a housemaid for the key."

"Very clever. Now you want to tell me what this is all about?"

Her eyes darted to the white envelope that lay propped against one of the gin glasses on the coffee table. I walked over and picked it up, being careful not to turn my back.

"What is it?" I asked. It was just a plain white envelope with no name or identifying mark on it.

She didn't answer me.

I tore it open and inside was a small chunk of plastic, not much bigger than the end of my index finger. In the light it looked like some kind of computer chip, one of those microprocessing circuits used in watches and calculators, only more elaborate.

"I don't get it," I said.

"It's a gift from my brother, Yoshitsune. He told me to tell you it's only a rough copy. The real thing is embedded in the skin of his chest. If you want it, you'll have to come fight him for it."

"I don't even know what it is."

"He said it was the key to your scrambler code."

I looked at it more carefully. It was definitely a

circuit of some kind, although you'd need a lab to tell you what it would be used for. According to her, this little hunk of plastic was capable of analyzing a voice print, assigning each point of it a numerical value, then scrambling the values according to the AXE code. It seemed like a tall order for something so small.

She must have guessed what I was thinking. "Don't discount little things," she said. "Sometimes it's the little things that are most important."

I sat down on the bed and pulled the phone over. "I have to make a call," I said, dialing with one hand while I held the gun on her with the other. Mattingly answered on the second ring.

"Our mysterious Lady of the Orient has put in a reappearance," I said.

"I see."

He hung up and I put the phone back on the table.

"Now, let me get this straight," I said, turning back to her. "Your brother. What's his name?"

"Yoshitsune."

"Yoshitsune Minamoto. Where've I heard that before?"

"In Japan he is considered a genius."

"Sure. Yoshitsune Minamoto, the computer genius. He's one of the men responsible for developing the micro-processing circuit to begin with."

"A mad genius, I'm afraid, Nick."

"That so?" I rolled the computer chip back and forth between my fingers, thinking. "What's he look like, this brother of yours?"

"He's smaller than you, broad shoulders . . ."

"Is he bald?"

"Yes."

"With lumps of scar tissue where his temples should be?"

"My brother has done extensive experimentation in electrode implantation. Unfortunately, his own brain was the only safe ground he could experiment on."

"Does he like to gamble?"

"Yes. He has a passion for it. He's made a great deal of money gambling. Nick, I can understand you have to ask me these questions, but can't you see how difficult it is for me?" Her eyelids beat back tears.

"What makes you say he's mad?"

"I don't know. He's changed. I hardly know him any more. When we were growing up, he was always so kind, so protective of me. He believed in the old samurai traditions. Then I went away to school in San Francisco and when I came back, he wouldn't even talk to me. It was as though I'd deserted him."

"Is that what made him mad?"

"I don't know what made him mad, but when I came home, he'd changed. He said the West made him sick, that Western culture had robbed Japan of everything that had made her great. It was crazy to listen to him. He'd get started and go on about it for hours. It got to the point where I was afraid to say anything to him at all for fear he'd launch into another of his tirades.

"And his work . . . He loved electronics. He used to sit me down and tell me of all the wonderful things it was possible to do, all the marvels he could create for mankind. I'd watch his face when he talked like that and it always excited me. He made it all sound so convincing . . . "

"But then that changed," I said.

"Yes. Shortly after I returned from the States he attended an international exposition in micro-electronics. He read a paper in front of the reviewing committee, stating publicly that the U.S. was responsible for most of the problems in Japan—our rising inflation rate, the softness of our youth, the drugs that infest our culture, the erosion of our old, better way of life. The paper was denounced as false and misleading, but there were a few who agreed with my brother.

"He went on to read other papers and to publish articles—all with the same anti-American theme. He became something of an embarrassment to his colleagues, I think. His work was discredited, even the originality of some of his inventions was questioned.

"Eventually, he became bitter, and instead of a passion, his work became an obsession. He became determined to show the world he was right. He started doing wild, dangerous things, like the electrodes he put in his brain. After a while, even his close friends deserted him. Now I'm the only one left who will go near him."

She was crying when she finished. Not out loud, but, her small shoulders were shaking with sobs. I put Wilhelmina down on the bed and waited for her to continue.

"I'm sorry," she said after a few minutes, pulling herself erect in the chair and daintily blowing her nose. "It's just that these last few months have been such a trial for both of us, my brother and me. He doesn't want to do the things he's doing, Nick. He's struggling to hold on to his sanity."

"I believe you," I said. I took a pack of my special brand of cigarettes from the night table and offered her one. She took it. I lit it with my lighter, then went back and sat on the bed while she tossed her mane of black hair and blew out a harried-looking jet of smoke.

"How did AXE get involved in all this? And why me?" I asked.

"A while ago my brother became interested in codes. He thought it might be a good way to harass the Americans. Then he started to amass a great deal of

money by gambling. He has a system that can't fail.
And with the money and what he'd learned about en-
coding procedures, he hit on another plan."

"What was that?"

"I don't know. He wouldn't discuss it with me.
About a year ago he started working in secret. Since
then I've only seen him intermittently. Once when he
asked me to go to Arizona and join the AXE staff, and
when he gave me the chip to bring here."

There was a knock at the door and I got up and
opened it. It was Mattingly, who came in wide-eyed,
taking everything in at a glance.

"She's all right," I told him. "It's her brother we
have to worry about."

He nodded, still looking at her. "What's your
name?" he asked abruptly.

"Gigi."

"Gigi, you mustn't leave in such a hurry next time.
You tend to make people suspicious. Especially, when
you forget your coat." He picked the stole off the arm
of the easy chair and handed it to her.

"Thank you," she said coldly. She took the fur and
wrapped it around her, then to me she said, "I wouldn't
want to lose it. It was a gift from Yoshitsune."

"That would be the brother," said Mattingly.

"That's right," I said.

Mattingly pulled up the easy chair so that we were all
sitting in a tight three-sided circle. "So, now that everything's out in the open and we're all such good friends,
maybe somebody would like to tell me what this is all
about."

I quickly explained to him what Gigi had told me
about her brother and the challenge he'd sent along with
the computer chip.

When I'd finished, Mattingly said, "So that's it. He wants to fight you. That's patently absurd."

"Why?"

"Why? Nick, old boy, you're not actually considering it?"

"I haven't decided. Why?"

"It's obviously a trap, and not particularly well-baited at that. We don't need this chip or whatever's embedded in this man's chest. The code's been deciphered. The entire system will have to be scrapped anyway."

"Wouldn't you like to know how it was done?"

"Not at the risk of my life. Or yours."

"Nick, both of you, please," Gigi interjected. "You're forgetting my brother is not a well man. He should be subdued without violence and taken somewhere he can get the rest and care he needs."

"Madam, excuse me," said Mattingly, turning on her, "but there is more at stake here than one man's sanity."

"All right, you two," I said. "John, maybe we should discuss this in private." I stood up and put Wilhelmina in her holster and stuffed the holster in my robe. Then I surveyed the room, trying to decide if it was all right to leave Gigi in here alone. "This won't take long," I told her. Then I motioned to Mattingly and we adjourned to the balcony.

I closed the glass doors behind us, but didn't lock them. He stood facing me with his back to the railing. "Keep an eye on her while we talk," I said.

"I thought you trusted her."

"I don't trust anyone, not even you. Now tell me, why are you opposed to this?"

"You're going to go, aren't you?"

"Yes."

"It's crazy. The man is a maniac and this time you might not be so lucky. I'm telling you it's a trap."

"Look, let me tell you something. I'm going to fight this man just the way he wants me to for two very good reasons. First, that chip may be valuable. I don't know. You don't know. I'm not a data-systems expert and neither are you.

"Second, Gigi's right. The man has to be stopped. There's no telling how much he's found out. Besides that, he's a homocidal maniac. This time he's managed to narrow his hatred to me alone. Next time the rest of the world might not be so lucky."

"I guess you're right," he conceded.

Mattingly and I had been looking directly at one another for several minutes. Finally, he glanced over my shoulder. "She's gone," he said.

Ten

Mattingly was the first one back in the room. There was no sign of her. He checked the bathroom while I searched the hall in both directions.

"That was stupid," I said when I came back in, referring to the fact I'd left her alone. "Still, I can't imagine why she'd leave."

"You don't know? I would say the lady is quite taken with you." Mattingly picked up a manila card that had been left on the coffee table and handed it to me. Written in a flowing hand was an address: 30 Rue de la Mer, number 14.

"Think this is a trap, too?" I asked, needling him a little.

"It wouldn't matter if it were. It doesn't do any good to warn you."

"I'll have to look into it," I said, putting the card in the pocket of my robe.

"Yes, I'm sure you will." From his tone it was clear he wasn't happy with this turn of events. He cleared his throat as a signal that he would be going. "I'll be leaving now. You're going through with this then?" he asked in reference to the fight with Minamoto.

"Yes."

"Very well. If I don't hear from you in thirty-six hours, I'll inform Washington."

"Right."

He walked to the door and turned around. "Good luck," he said. Then he opened it and left.

I locked the door behind him, took off my robe and started to dress. I strapped Wilhelmina into her familiar spot under my arm and tightened the buckles on Hugo's chamois case. I flexed my arm to make sure he was secure, then I grabbed my cashmere jacket and left.

Thirty Rue de la Mer was only a short cab ride away, a Spanish style oblong apartment building right in the center of town. By the time I got there it was after ten o'clock. I paid the driver and started up the shrubbery-lined sidewalk to the front door.

Around me the Monacan night-life hummed. Couples ambled aimlessly up and down the boulevard. The air was damp and smelled faintly of salt. I realized that although I'd been in town over twenty-four hours, this was the first time I'd been out in the city and it all seemed a trifle disorienting.

I opened the door to the front vestibule, went in, and pushed the button for number fourteen.

"Who is it?" asked a tiny voice over the intercom.

"Nick."

The door buzzed and I went up. Gigi answered when I knocked on her door, wearing a kimono. She didn't say anything. I came in and she bustled past me into the kitchen. She had pinned her hair on the top of her head and from the back you could see the soft, luxuriant black shadow at the nape of her neck.

While she was gone, I took a quick look around. It was a modest apartment, although in Monte Carlo even a lean-to is expensive. The furniture had come with the place, the kind that usually does, but she'd added a touch here and there to make it seem more like home. A scroll painting hung on one wall and there was a spare Japanese flower arrangement in a rectangular pot in the corner.

In the center of the room the furniture had been pushed back and a low, black-lacquered wood table was surrounded by cushions for kneeling. On the table was a tea service for two.

She came into the room carrying a small tray with a fragile-looking white stoneware teapot on it. "Please sit down," she said.

I remembered my manners and slipped off my shoes. Then I kneeled at the table and waited while she poured the tea. I knew from previous trips to Japan what a great deal of importance they placed on the ceremony of drinking tea. To the Japanese it is more than a polite conversational gesture; it is a sacred ritual, a rite that if performed correctly can heal the social wounds between two people.

She poured tea into two tiny cups and handed one to me.

"These are very beautiful cups," I said, remembering it always polite to praise the china.

"They are very old. They have been in my family over four hundred years."

We drank. When we put down our cups, I opened with a trump. "You left my room in a hell of a hurry this evening. We were a little surprised to find you gone."

"It was that man."

"Mattingly?"

"I don't think he intended to help my brother."

"Perhaps not, but he's not a bad man really; he's just suspicious for obvious reasons."

She didn't answer.

I rolled my tea cup back and forth on the table in front of me, absently staring at the pattern of tea leaves strewn on the bottom. "I don't know if I can help your brother either," I said. "If it comes down to it, I may have to kill him."

What I said hung in the air like a stale odor. It took a long time for her to speak. For several seconds she stared into a corner of the room, then said, "If it has to be done, I'm glad you were the one chosen to do it."

I made no answer to this, and in a few minutes she arranged the cups and tea pot on the tray and carried them out to the kitchen.

Several more minutes passed. She didn't return and I couldn't hear her. I was on the verge of getting up and going into the other room to see if anything was wrong, when she came back with another tray, this time with a pack of expensive English cigarettes, an ashtray, and a brightly-decorated pack of wooden matches.

She set the tray down on the table, then knelt at an angle, turning only her profile to me. The skin of her cheeks glistened with tears.

"In my country years ago," she began, "when men and women of the high-born class were not allowed to mingle, it was sometimes difficult for a girl to speak directly to a man. She would turn her head, as I am doing now, so that she could not see whether the words that came from her heart made him angry or pleased him.

"We met under a false pretense, you and I. My brother forged my security clearance and got me a position on the AXE staff so that I could meet you and challenge you to a karate match. The purpose I was told was to test you to see if you were worthy of fighting my brother. I was not supposed to fall in love with you.

"But who can possibly predict these things? If you hadn't been so gallant in accepting my challenge, or made me ache so with desire to look at you, our sparring contest might not have come to such an abrupt and unexpected conclusion.

"Now in a few hours you'll be fighting with Yoshitsune, trying to kill one another. And whichever of the two of you wins, I lose."

At this point she broke into tears and couldn't stop. I got up and came around to her side of the table, knelt down and held her. She made no effort to stop crying; she let it flow. "I just wanted you to understand," she said between gulps, "why I acted the way I did at the hotel. I couldn't face you."

She buried her head in my shoulder and sobbed, convulsing like a tiny wounded bird. I ran my hand down her long black hair. We stayed like this for several minutes while she cried and cried.

Finally, it seemed as though she'd spent it all. She was like a baby crying itself to sleep, only she wasn't asleep. She lay in my arms silently for a few minutes, then she pulled back and looked at me.

"Make love to me, Nick," she said.

I kissed her. It wasn't like it had been before. She was all emotion now. There was no restraint, no holding back out of fear. She yielded to me and engulfed me at the same time.

I opened her kimono. Her skin was warm. I buried my head between her breasts and her arms reached up and encircled me. She was crying again.

"Don't stop. Please," she whispered. I didn't intend to and quickly undressed.

I kissed her stomach. She was beginning to make low

moaning sounds in her throat. It was a beautiful throat. I reached up and kissed that, too.

Her breathing was coming faster and faster, but I went on kissing and stroking, telling myself to be patient, to wait until she ached for me. But the truth was I didn't want to stop. Each movement was a communication between us, a message relayed and understood.

Finally I entered her, a long, slow surge. She gripped my shoulders and gasped.

After that, it was like a swim in a river of forgetfulness. I stopped thinking and lost myself in feeling. It wasn't anything like what it had been in Phoenix. After battling one another for almost an hour, our lovemaking had been explosive, torrid. Now it was gentle, full of consideration for the other.

Every time she moved, she taught me something new about her body, some new way to excite her. I rubbed against her, fell back, came forward. Everything was new as though I'd never done it before.

Eventually, I felt the first hints of those familiar forces building in my lower body. The peak was coming. I fought it, wanting it and not wanting it at the same time. Finally it overtook me whether I wanted it to or not, and I slammed my body against her's with amazing force. I crossed the threshold and hung in midair for what seemed an eternity, then fell, pumping, pumping, floating down, down, until I was adrift on a perfectly calm sea.

She'd reached her peak at exactly the same moment, grabbed me and shrieked, then let herself go. Now we were enmeshed in one another. I couldn't tell where her body ended and mine began.

We lay still a long while. I didn't open my eyes until I felt her stir. We were on the floor. The table had been pushed aside and the cushions scattered.

I rolled over on my back and she rolled on top of me, clinging to me. I rocked her back and forth in my arms like a child until she relaxed. She swallowed hard and I knew from her face that she was her composed self again. She knew what had to be done and she'd resigned herself to it.

Still neither of us wanted to move. She began kissing my arms and neck. She stopped when she came to the blue, black, and yellow bruise on the side of my rib cage.

"How did that happen?" she asked, touching it tenderly with the tips of her fingers.

"Your brother."

She nodded, then rolled off me, pulled her kimono around herself and sat up.

"Where do I find him?" I asked.

She pulled her knees up to her chin and rested her head. She looked like finely chiseled marble. "I don't want to tell you."

"You're going to have to."

She got to her feet suddenly and walked to a desk set against the wall. She pulled out a sheet of paper, wrote on it quickly, then came back and handed it to me.

"He bought a mansion out along the coast. It used to be a French villa, but he's remodeled it. There's a big wooden gate. You can't miss it." She said this without the slightest twinge of feeling.

I opened the sheet. The address was on it. I folded it back up again.

"You're going now? How can you make love to me, then turn around and go out and try and kill my brother?"

I couldn't say anything. I just looked at her.

"Don't answer. Go. Go on," she said, a note of weariness in her voice.

I stood up, gathered my clothes, and began dressing. It took awhile. I had Wilhelmina to strap on. I hadn't bothered to remove Hugo. He was still attached to my arm.

She stared at me sadly from the floor. It was as though she didn't have any feeling left.

I took my jacket and was about to leave. "Nick!" she burst out as I headed to the door. She ran up and threw her arms around me, pressing her body against mine. The smell of her hair, the smooth feel of her back under my hands started that old tension deep in my gut. I wanted her again.

"Please, don't. Don't," she sobbed.

I pulled her arms from around my neck and looked sternly into her face. Then I gently lifted her chin with my finger. Her lip was quivering. I kissed it, then I turned and walked out the door.

Eleven

I took a cab back to the hotel and went down below to the underground parking lot to get the Porsche out. The attendant's cage was locked, however, with a sign in the window telling me in French, English, and German that after eleven thirty keys were kept upstairs at the front desk.

I took the elevator to the first floor, crossed the practically deserted lobby and presented my parking stub to the young man on duty. He memorized the number and disappeared into a small office behind the desk. When he returned, he had my keys in one hand and an envelope in the other.

"This came for you while you were out, Monsieur."

"Thank you," I said.

I recrossed the lobby and pressed the button for the elevator. While I waited, I opened the envelope and read.

There were two sheets. One was a note from Mattingly. The other was a telex addressed with the usual

Amalgamated Press cover, indicating it was confidential from Hawk's office, but not with enough priority to be coded. I read the telex first.

It was headed, "RE: Analysis Object #537010." Object #537010, I remembered, was the plastic film cartridge I'd found in the apartment in Ann Arbor. I'd sent it into the lab while I was in Washington and it had taken all this time to catch up to me.

The body of the report was mostly technical: a breakdown of the plastic used, the date and location of manufacture, a list of possible outlets where it might have been purchased. At the bottom it said, "PROBABLE USE: casette insert for Bashe IF100 16mm motion picture film." The letters "IF" had been underlined by Hawk, in red ink as usual.

I folded the report and stuck it in my jacket pocket, thinking I'd digest it later. Then I read the note from Mattingly. It was nothing, just an introduction to the telex, saying he'd received it through channels and was passing it along. I crumbled it up and threw it in a trash barrel as I was walking through the lot.

The significance of Hawk's underline didn't hit me until fifteen minutes later while I was in the Porsche breezing through the streets of downtown Monte Carlo. "IF" stood for infra-red. The entire episode in the basement of that house had been photographed in the dark using infra-red film. But why?

I went through the checkpoint that separates Monaco from France, took a left and started climbing the brief hill that would take me out of town.

There are two main highways running between Monte Carlo and Nice: La Grande Cornishe, the one I took in from the airport, which skirts the edges of the cliffs eight hundred feet above the shoreline and is considered spectacular if too dangerous for general use;

and La Petite Cornishe, a more recent road mostly for the benefit of commuters, which is cut through the jagged rocks closer to the ocean. The address Gigi gave me was located roughly halfway to Nice off La Petite Cornishe.

I came up a rise into a narrow place between two outcroppings of rock where the road curved away from the sea. On the other side was an auxiliary road leading down to the shore, over the entrance of which was a massive wooden arch in the shape of a pagoda. She was right. You couldn't miss it.

I took a left and drove down about a hundred yards until I found an opening in the wall of thick shrubbery that bordered the drive. I pulled into the bushes, turned off the lights, and cut the engine. Then I slipped out and closed the car door as tightly as I could without slamming it.

These precautions were no doubt a waste of time. In all probability I was expected down below just as I had been in Ann Arbor and aboard St. Germaine's yacht, but old habits die hard.

I walked down the remainder of the drive. The full moon created shadows on the asphalt like a midday sun. There was a fierce switch-back, then a gradual curve, and the driveway leveled out and ended in a broad parking area in front of a four-door garage.

I walked to the edge of the parking area and peered over the waist-high, stone retaining wall that surrounded it. Below me, down eighty feet of sheer rock face, the surf roiled in the crags. Looking toward the house and on up the coast the breaking waves created a necklace of silver in the moon's light.

The house itself abutted the sea on a foundation of solid rock and in the moonlight looked big enough to bivouac a regiment. Gigi was right. Obviously, at one time it had been a millionaire's villa done in the usual French style. The one wall visible to me, the one facing the sea, had six towering, windowed french doors that opened onto a courtyard balcony.

But the millionaire who built it would never recognize it now. Not only had a number of floors been added, but the roofline had been completely changed to fit in with the peculiar tastes of its new owner. The eaves of the original squared-off mansard roof had been enlarged and turned upward so the entire structure looked like a giant pagoda. It was the same style of architecture used in the ancient Japanese castles where shoguns once cloistered the imperial family like a collection of prize butterflies. In fact, as I looked at the house, I could almost imagine I was back in seventeenth-century Osaka, staring up at the western wall of the fortress as the sea crashed against the outer walls below.

Fortress or not, I still had to figure out some way to get inside. I crossed the parking lot and began pushing my way through the shrubbery, trying to encircle the landward side of the house as far as I could.

I hadn't gone more than a hundred yards when I came upon a high voltage pylon planted in the rocks. In the moonlight I could see two more stretching back up to the highway, carrying a number of heavy-hanging wires over the high stone wall into the house. Whatever Minamoto was doing in there, it required a good deal of electricity. I pushed on another few dozen feet and ran smack into a blank rock cliff and had to turn around.

Once back in the parking lot I realized I had only two possibilities. There was a door on one end of the garage which, although unobtrusive, was obviously the way one would enter the house. Or I could climb out along the retaining wall above the water, jump down into the courtyard and try my luck with one of the big french doors.

I chose the french doors, thinking that would be the way he'd least expect me, and climbed the wall where it met the wall of the garage. There was space enough to inch my way along, maybe a hand's span or two, but there was nothing to hold on to but the smooth wall of the garage. The sea pounded below me, and now and then the up-draft brought a misting of spray to give me a foretaste of what would happen if I slipped.

At the far end of the garage wall, I ran into a far more perilous obstacle. A space of several yards divided the rear of the garage and the courtyard, and for two or three steps I'd have to be tightrope walking without so much as a pole to balance myself; and the wind out here was a good deal more vicious than it had been back at the parking lot.

As I stepped out cautiously, leaving the garage wall behind, the wind roared and whipped my pants against my legs. It did its insidious best to knock me off the few inches of solidity I stood up on, blowing me hard toward the house—forcing me to compensate in that direction—then stopping all of a sudden, so that my attempt to balance myself almost toppled me into the sea.

I took a step, then another. Again the wind shifted, pushing me from the rear. I went down on one knee, but the knee missed the top of the wall and I slid off, the edge of the rocks scrapping along my side.

I hung on for dear life by my hands, my feet dangling over eighty feet of nothingness. I had to pull myself up, throw a leg over the top somehow, but that meant pressure on my hand grip, and on the wind-and-water-smoothed rocks my fingers were already starting to separate and disengage.

The only thing left was to swing back and forth and build up some momentum. I pulled to the left, and when I swung back to the right, I strained and shot out my leg. My knee hit the stones a half foot below the top and I fell back.

I hung there for a minute, trying to think, the wind screaming in my ears. After that last effort my hands had slipped an inch closer to disaster. I had to try again, but this time I couldn't afford to fall short.

I swung to the left, then to the right, then back to the left again, the pain in my hands telling me how desperate this was. I came back to the right as hard as possible, threw my knee and missed, but managed to catch on with my foot. With that added hold I was able to pull the knee and with it the rest of my body back over the ridge, until I was in a straddle position on top of the wall.

I shinnied along, keeping flat, until my right foot hit the wall surrounding the courtyard. Then I threw my leg over and let myself down, dropping into the shrubbery.

I lay there a minute, listening for sounds of having awakened anyone. No one came but the roar of the ocean and the wind.

The courtyard was empty and the moonlight on the white gravel gave it an eerie, unearthly quality. I got up and walked across to the six black oblongs the french doors made in the side of the house. Carefully, I tried the second from the end. It was locked. I cupped my hands and peered through the pane, but could see nothing inside.

I checked the rest of the doors and found all locked; then I went back to the second door. The lock was one of those that are so simple, they defy the burglar's art. There was no keyhole, just a brass deadbolt thrown with latch from the other side.

I had no choice. I found a hefty stone, covered it with

my handkerchief, tapped on one of the panes until it broke, and waited for the alarm bell.

The surf pounded, the wind hummed above the courtyard, and that was all.

I opened the door and slipped in. The moonlight streamed through the panes of the glass doors and fell in rectangular patterns across a wide floor of checkerboard tiles. I slipped Wilhelmina out of her holster and hurried toward the opposite wall. The room was large; at one time it might have been used as a ballroom or dining hall. Now, as far as I could see, it was empty.

When I reached the other side, I pressed my back flat against a door where light was visible through the cracks. I waited a few seconds, then pulled it open.

Through the door was a hallway, although not the kind you'd expect to find in a house. It was more like a corridor in an office building—empty. The walls were painted a uniform, sterile gray, and the ceiling was lit with a series of square florescent light fixtures.

I came out cautiously, pulling the door shut behind me. The hall ran in three directions, to my right, my left, and straight ahead. In each wall were doors spaced every few feet. I chose the right, walked down a way and tried the first door. It was locked. I tried another on the other side. It was locked, too.

After I'd tried the second one, I realized there was something strange about both these doors. They didn't rattle in their jambs the way a door will when it isn't fit exactly snug into its frame. They were immovable. It made me wonder if they were really doors at all, or just knobs screwed in place.

I tried several more, all with the same result. When I came to the end of the hall I turned around and went back to my starting point. Out of curiosity, I tried the door I'd just come through. It wouldn't budge.

I shook it. The knob began to come loose, but the door stood solid as an oak. Flexing my wrist, I ejected Hugo into the palm of my hand. Over the years he's gotten me through a lot of doors. I inserted his needle point into the lock in an effort to separate the tumblers, only he wouldn't go in. I bent down and discovered the reason why. The keyhole was plugged with steel.

I shook the door again, but it was like trying to pry a rock out of a sheer stone cliff. I was locked in. If I was going to get out, it wasn't going to be this way.

But I decided I couldn't worry about that now. There was a bigger question: Did the fact the door was locked mean someone knew I was here, or had it locked automatically when I shut it?

I was standing there, running this through my mind, my hand still on the knob, when something happened that made me wonder if I were seeing right: The corridor-wall directly in front of me began to move.

Silently, fluidly, the end of the hall came forward a full fifteen feet and then stopped. Then another section to the left fell away, forming another wholly new branch to the corridor.

I was dumbfounded. After a few seconds the maneuver was complete and everything stopped. I waited a few anxious seconds to see if anything else would happen, then I went down to examine the new section.

It was nothing, a dead end like the others, with doors spaced at intervals on either side. I tried one, but it wouldn't open—as I'd much suspected would be the case. I checked the joint where the two walls came together. The seal was perfect. If I hadn't seen it happen, I'd never have known.

This brought up the possibility that maybe the walls had shifted earlier while I was testing the doors and I hadn't seen them. Then the door I thought was the one I used to come in might not have been that door at all. Maybe it was another door and I wasn't locked in.

I started back to where I'd been standing before the walls began to move, came around the corner and stopped short. The entire partition at the far end where I'd been, doors and all, disappeared as another section rolled in and sealed the area off. If I had any doubts about being trapped in here, they evaporated.

At the same time a section moved at the opposite end of the new corridor I'd just been examining, thus opening another extension. So there was a method in all this. I was being led in a specific direction like a rat in a maze, and I had no choice but to go along.

I walked down the new corridor, my finger nervously working against Wilhelmina's trigger. I thought I heard something behind me and I turned around in time to see the sections of corridor closing in the rear. In front of me new sections were opening up.

Twelve

I proceeded this way for several hundred feet, although there were never more than ten yards of hallway open at any one time. As I approached the end of the ten yards, the wall in front of me would pull back and the section behind me would close.

Then it occurred to me to run a little experiment. I stopped altogether and sat down with my back against the left-hand lateral wall. The movements of the partition in front and behind ceased. Minutes went by, and they stood silently waiting. I had the feeling they would wait forever if I didn't move.

I stood up and started walking again, only this time I varied my pace. I slowed down, then sped up, and with each change of speed, the walls compensated. This led me to believe they were probably being operated by computer, which meant the machine must have some device for sensing where I was, most likely in the overhead lighting.

As I walked along, I considered shooting out a string

of the overheads to see what would happen. I weighed this against the two clips of ammunition I'd brought, trying to decide, when I was again caught me completely by surprise.

Instead of moving out and away, leaving me a straight passage in which to move, the forward wall stopped and the walls on either side fell back, presenting me with two directions to follow rather than one.

I stopped in the intersection and looked down each hall. They both went for the same distance. In fact, they were identical; there was nothing to indicate whether I should go one way or the other.

"Which way?" I shouted. My voice echoed against the smooth surface of the walls and died away. There was no answer.

This is absurd, I thought; but which way?

I turned to the right. The wall at the end of the corridor began to recede in front of me and I could hear the left-hand hall rolling shut behind me, sealing that possibility forever.

I continued on for the better part of an hour, making numerous turns. I didn't think I was being led in circles, but I couldn't be sure. Four times I was given the option as to which direction to go, twice with choices ahead or behind, twice with the decision of turning left or going on straight ahead. Each time I took the way I thought would lead me further into the interior of the building.

Finally, the inevitable happened, the ploy I'd been waiting for since I found out the walls were movable. I turned a corner and came down a straight section of hallway, expecting the wall in front of me to ebb away as it had been doing all along. Only this time it didn't. It just stood there like the blunt end of a giant hammer.

The wall behind me continued to close in.

I'd given some thought to what I would do if this happened. The walls didn't move all that fast. It had occurred to me that it might be possible, if I were very quick, to shinny up the space between them and make an escape into the ceiling by knocking out the overhead. There would have to be a crawl space up there of some kind to house the wiring and mechanisms necessary for a set-up like this.

Of course, this was assuming I was healthy, which I wasn't, and not fatigued, which I was fast becoming at two-thirty in the morning after a night of very little sleep.

The wall crept toward me, foot by foot. I holstered Wilhelmina and braced myself. Twenty feet away, then fifteen. There wasn't going to be much time.

Five feet. I lifted my leg to catch the wall as it came. It moved in big and blank, growing bigger. I looked up at the ceiling, and it seemed a mile away. I asked myself how in the world I ever hoped to scramble up this blank mountain all that way using only the forward wall as a support?

I felt weak suddenly, my body telling me I'd already pushed it to the limit. There wasn't enough left in me to crawl that fast that far. I couldn't do it.

I dropped my foot. The wall rolled in and pressed against my body. Like some brute rapist, the cold steel kissed my cheek. The overhead was out now, the wall having moved beyond it, and the pinched space left to me was dark.

I didn't want to give up. My mind kept racing, looking for a possible escape. There had to be some way.

The wall pressed its case. I could feel the rivets

where the sheets of it were spliced together and even the criss-cross of the support rods on which the metal sheets were hung.

My feet splayed out duck-style and the first bolts of pain shot up from my unnaturally twisted knees.

Soon my ankles, knees, hips, shoulders, all felt it. The air rushed out of my lungs in a wheezing moan that at first I couldn't believe had come from me. The wall, pressed flat against the side of my face, ground into my cheekbones, my ears, and the back of my head.

A crazy fear ran through my mind. I was afraid my body would be crushed, but not my skull. Then I wouldn't die, at least not right away, but the bones and the splinters would skewer everything in me. I didn't think I could stand that kind of pain.

I was about to go limp, realizing resistence only made it hurt more and that I would never be able to make myself disappear completely, when the wall to my rear suddenly opened up and I fell backwards into darkness.

I lay for a few seconds without trying to get up, then pulled myself slowly to my feet. My joints ached but nothing seemed to be broken. Still, I was shaking. For a minute I thought that, after all these years, I'd finally had it.

Everything still in total darkness, I groped my way back to the wall and the place where I'd fallen through. It was gone. I searched for several yards in either direction, but I couldn't find any evidence of a door, or even a seam.

I decided to begin walking to my right, running one hand along the wall, counting my paces. Thirty-two steps later I still hadn't made contact with an adjoining wall or anything else, when a bright light flashed on and there was a snap and a surging sound like an electric motor being started.

There was also a loud hissing noise like a steam valve being blown off time and again. I shaded my eyes and squinted into the glare. What I saw was unbelievable. Towering above me was a mechanial reproduction of a medieval Chinese dragon. It was huge, over twelve feet high, and out from between the shoulder blades of its stubby, dinosaur-like body shot eight long necks like snakes, and at the end of each of these was a snake's head, hissing and darting its tongue.

I recoiled half a step in amazement. Minamoto had done a superb job of animation. Never had I seen anything fabricated out of metal, cloth, and plastic look so real. Saliva dripped from the snakes' mouths, and its outer covering glinted with blue and gold like the prismatic scales of a fish. Even the nostrils flared as though they were actually sucking air.

I was so astounded, I forgot to be careful. Out of nowhere, one of the heads, half a foot from eye to eye, and a foot and a half long, swooped down and snagged my leg with the fangs that protruded five inches from its upper jaw. It tore my trousers and opened a bloody slash in my shin, and then it snapped back like lightning.

I pulled out Wilhelmina. For a few seconds I followed the head trying to get a clear shot, then took a bead on one of its brothers. The heads whipped back and forth like striking pythons, never lingering in one spot long enough to gun down. Finally, I held the gun steady and waited for a head to move into line. Then I squeezed off a shot.

I got one under the back part of the jaw, but except for a slight jarring, the bullet had no effect whatever.

I fired again. This time it went into one of the eyes. The eye popped like a picture tube. A pale wisp of smoke came out of the empty socket and the jaw dropped open, although the neck went on flailing the air like the others.

Knocking out one of the heads only seemed to anger it. Another head sailed at me, hitting the wall behind me with a sickening thud when I ducked just in time.

No sooner had I stood up again than another pair of jaws smacked the floor in front of me. I jumped and tried to come down on top of it, but I was way late. When I recovered my balance, I trained Wilhemina on it, thinking I'd blow it off its neck, but it had recoiled by this time and I didn't want to waste a shot.

While I was concentrating on that one, another struck from behind. They were coming at me snake-fashion, from all directions, lunging fangs first, trying to hook them into me.

I side-stepped the threat to the rear, swung and caught it between the eyes with the butt of the Luger. Again, I had to marvel at Minamoto's programming. The head sprung back as though it were actually hurt.

So far I'd been lucky, but so far it had only been toying with me. I was too close to it. But every time I tried to move out of the way, another snake head cut me off. I batted at them with Wilhelmina whenever one came close, but I didn't kid myself into thinking I was doing any damage.

Then I saw an opportunity to make a run for it. Six of the heads arched back simultaneously, testing the air with their tongues, allowing themselves to coordinate the attack so they didn't all run into one another. This left two down low to keep me busy. One of these was the head I'd shot out earlier.

My first instinct was to rush the weaker side, but that

would leave my back unprotected, and the weak head, while it couldn't bite me, could act as a barrier while the second moved in for the kill. So I feinted in the direction of the fully functional head, two steps, as though I were going to make a break.

It thought it had me. Out of the corner of my eye, I saw it timing its attack to intercept me in motion.

It struck, and this time it wasn't fooling. It came flying hard and fast. I sucked in my chest. The head whizzed past close enough to brush the lapels of my coat, then hit the wall with a crack and broke off both its fangs. It recoiled a hell of a lot slower than it had charged and I took off for the other side of the room.

The room's decor was every bit as strange as the dragon. It was like a stage set. Piled waist high along the floor were masses of raw cotton set out in blob-like shapes. The floor, walls, and ceiling had been painted in variegated hues to resemble a blue sky, azure at the base and growing gradually paler to almost pure white at the top. In the ceiling burned an electric imitation sun, and along the walls and hung midway between floor and ceiling on wires were additional masses of cotton, supposedly to resemble clouds.

The idea I gathered was that the dragon and I were supposed to be fighting somewhere in midair high above the earth. I hadn't the vaguest notion as to why Minamoto would go to all this trouble just to create an effect, but the cotton at floor level was the only cover available, so I plunged in.

When I got to the middle, I crouched down and pushed away the cotton that obscured my view of the dragon. Then I framed him in my sights.

He moved toward me on his back legs, dragging his ponderous tail behind him. Because of his enormity he only had to go a few steps to have me cornered. I was going to have to stay on the run, constantly shifting positions to keep ahead of him and avoid being stabbed to death by those knife-like fangs.

Before he got too close, I fired. The bullet ricocheted off one of the necks and struck a wall. I fired again and hit a head dead center. It jerked upward, then fell back into its original position, still operational. Apparently, I'd been lucky the first time around and found the one chink in its armor, the eyes.

I took more careful aim and squeezed. Wilhelmina kicked a little in my hand and I missed the eye by a few inches.

He was closing in. In a few seconds I was going to have to run for it. I pulled the trigger again and this time, in one of the longer-necked heads, the eye went black and glass tinkled to the floor. The neck still moved, but the head itself was out of commission.

I saw a glint in the light above me and ducked down just as a pair of fangs shot past my head. Another followed close behind.

I scrambled to my feet and started running along the wall. When I came to another white patch, I trampled my way into the center of it, crouched and got myself ready again.

Two heads down with six shots. Three bullets left in the gun and nine more in the spare clip. I couldn't afford to waste any.

The dragon spun around, whipping its huge tail and crashed it into the far wall. That was something else I was going to have to keep an eye on. If he caught me with that tail, I was a goner.

The heads sawed the air, hissing. They were looking for me. Finally, one of them spotted my hiding place and they all trained on it.

I drew a bead on another eye and fired. Missed. Too
far away and moving too fast.

I aimed again, holding the old girl steady at arm's
length and using my left hand for support. I fired and
missed, then fired again in quick succession. The second bullet found its mark and another eye went black,
the head becoming nothing but dead weight.

Clearly I had to move again. I shot past his back leg
just ahead of a flying pair of fangs, then jumped to
avoid the backlashing of the tail. I went up and it went
under, but my rear foot hit, flipping me. I fell on my
side, rolled, and came up running.

When I was out of range of those needle teeth, I
stopped. The spare clip was in my inside pocket. I dug it
out and slammed it into the butt of the Luger. Then I
hunkered down and took aim.

Thirteen

The dragon had already turned and was coming for me. I fired six more times and took out two more heads. When he flushed me from the cotton again and I circled the perimeter of the room until I was behind him. Then I got down and took aim once again.

So far this little game was working to my advantage. Except for one small problem: I was running out of ammo. I had three heads left, one of which had smashed the teeth out of itself earlier. But I had only three more bullets, and my score to date, bullets vs. heads, wasn't the best.

As the dragon turned to move toward my new position, I noticed something about it that had escaped me before. Between its legs, running from its body to a hole in the floor, was a thick black cable.

How could I have been so stupid? I wondered. Here was the way to defeat this thing. Simply cut off its power source.

Before the dragon could turn to face me, I started

moving again, circling the room. The dragon was forced to spin with me to keep me in front of him. He was built in such a way that he had to dip his body in order for the heads to strike at me, and the only way he could do that was forward.

Unfortunately for him, he couldn't spin as fast as I could circle. Eventually, I got around behind him and had a clear shot at the cable. I crouched and fired. I could have sworn I'd hit it, but nothing happened. Clearly I was going to have to get closer.

I circled again until I had him facing the opposite way, then charged his rear. He swung his lanced tail at me, trying to swat me like a fly, but I was ready for it and dodged out of the way. Then I quickly ran in close to the base of it before he could whip it toward me again, and put my hand on its haunch to steady myself.

The dragon reared and clawed the air with his smaller front feet. The hissing increased in ferocity as he kept trying to turn around and crush me. I held the gun three feet from the cable and fired.

The bullet made a white mark where it deflected off the black plastic sheathing but failed to penetrate. I fired again and a second white mark appeared like a twin to the first. I had used up all my ammunition.

Hissing noises above me indicated what lay in store. The heads were striking, but I was still just out of range. I holstered the gun and ejected Hugo. Then I turned to face them with the only weapon I had left.

A head sprung at me. I pulled back out of its path to let it shoot by, grabbed it by the neck in a bear hug before it could recoil, and jumped on for a ride.

The mechanism was stronger than I thought. It shipped me through the air as though an extra hundred and eighty pounds were nothing at all. At first it was all I could do to hold on, but when I figured I'd seen the full range of its efforts to throw me, I pulled myself aboard like a bronco rider.

I grabbed the head by the snout, one hand around the upper jaw between the fangs, reared back, and plunged Hugo into the eye. The glass broke and the head dropped, lowering the fangs. The change was so sudden, I had to hold on with both hands to keep from falling off.

The ride wasn't over though—not by a long shot. The neck began swinging back and forth like a pendulum, building speed. Then it heaved back and snapped me across the room. I hit the wall with my back about eight feet above the floor and fell.

For a minute I just lay there. Everything hurt. That was one rodeo stunt I wouldn't be doing again soon.

I could hear it moving toward me, its big, clawed feet scraping the floor, but I couldn't move. When I finally looked up, it was right over me, a big scaly mass of stomach with tendrils that seemed to reach to the ceiling.

Two fangs dived toward me, hit the wall just above my head and glanced off, slicing part of my arm in the process.

The sight of blood was enough to bring me back to my senses. I crawled out from between the wall and the dragon, got my feet under me somehow and ran for safety. I didn't stop until I was flat against the far wall. I let it hold me up, panting, the air moving in and out of my lungs like a wood rasp.

This last little adventure had turned the corner for me. I was exhausted. I'd put about everything I had into this fight and still hadn't been able to beat this thing.

I tried to think of some strategy, but my mind wouldn't function anymore. All I could do was stare. The dragon made one final turn, located my position, and came stalking in my direction.

Most of the heads beat the air spastically, slack-jawed, running into one another like a machine gone berserk. Three of them, however, two with teeth, rode on the beast's shoulders looking down at me soberly. Apparently, I'd created a short in the head I'd just disabled with Hugo. Sparks flew from its mouth, and instead of hissing, it popped.

I watched it come, wondering if I had the strength to elude it again, fast coming to the conclusion I didn't, when a panel opened in the wall only a few feet from me and a small platform extended.

On the platform, ensconced on a red velvet pad, was an ornate sword, the kind once used by the ancient samurai.

I looked over at it with a measure of wonder and disgust. What was Minamoto up to, anyway? I asked myself. How long was he going to toy with me? First the maze, then the dragon, now this.

The dragon was pressing. The closer of the three working heads had already coiled and was getting ready to strike. I ran over, grabbed the sword, and moved clear.

The dragon spun around, swishing its tail into the little platform, splintering it and sending the red velvet cushion flying.

I unsheathed the sword. It was the real thing. Etched on the tip of the blade was the *horimono*, the hallmark of the craftsman who made it. I tried it a few times. It hummed in the air. These swords weren't like the brittle cutlasses and rapiers made in Europe. The Japanese developed a process of pounding the metal out and folding it back on itself thousands of times, strengthening the blade far beyond the tolerance of a single-forged piece of steel. In the hands of a master a sword like this could fell a tree.

The new weapon in my hands rejuvenated me. The dragon moved in, but I stood my ground, letting him get dangerously close. I waited until he was towering over me, the monstrous snake pit between his shoulders coiling and uncoiling. Then I swung with all my might.

The sword hit one of the necks of the nonfunctioning heads inches below the line where the neck and head joined, sunk an inch or so into whatever material covered the dragon's frame, then bounced off as though the blade were made of rubber.

I swung again hitting the shoulder from which the necks sprouted, hoping to relieve this thing of all eight heads in one blow. Same result. The sword sprang off, twisting me halfway in the other direction on the rebound.

A head struck at me from above. I fended it off with my arm, but the force of it almost knocked me over. A second attacked from the other side. They had me in a crossfire.

I swung the sword furiously to clear them away. When they retreated, I lunged at the dragon's body, trying to drive the point through its chest. It wouldn't penetrate. I tried again and couldn't get the swordpoint past the slimy outer covering. Something was preventing it.

Then it dawned on me: The whole dragon must have been covered with the same black plastic as the cable in back. I didn't know what that plastic was, but it was the toughest material I'd ever tried to go through.

By this time the heads were on me again, sailing at me from both directions. I made a swoop with the sword that sounded like the wing stroke of a giant bird.

They backed off and I got away again.

On the other side of the room, I was at my wit's end. I had no idea why I had been given the sword since it did me no good. I was about to fling it across the room, when suddenly something clicked in my mind.

The handle of the sword was thickly coated with rubber, something a samurai would obviously never use. At first I'd thought it was for improving the grip. But now I wondered if perhaps it weren't there to insulate its user against electrical shock.

If this were true, did it mean Minamoto was deliberately hinting at a way out of this mess?

I didn't stop to analyze the implications of this. I took Hugo in my right hand and the sword in my left and ran around to the rear of the dragon.

Again, he tried to dispose of me with his tail. I waited while he swung it back to get leverage, then rushed in before he could whiplash it around and catch me.

This time I didn't bide my time in the protective hollow of his backside. I jumped on his spine using Hugo like a climber's piton, digging him into the outer covering, pulling myself up, then plunging him in again.

The heads spotted me coming up the back and the three still functioning went wild trying to stop me. They flew back and forth in a frenzy, hissing like a colony of adders. But the robot was designed to attack facing forward. Consequently, the line of flight necessary to get a good strike at me was a little awkward.

One head flew at me and fell half a foot short, stabbing its own body near the shoulder blades with its fangs. These caught in the covering material until the head jerked them free and recoiled for another try.

I realized as long as I stayed plastered against the back of it, I was fairly safe. But I hadn't come this far to be cozy. Using Hugo, I inched up the neck of the head that had thrown me earlier. It was still sputtering like a volcano.

I made it to within a foot of the head itself, hanging like a kid on a thin branch in a windstorm, when another of the necks suddenly wrapped itself around the base of the one I was on. I could see what was coming. They began to entwine like two mating snakes with me in the middle.

Snake bodies would have been tolerable. At least they would have had some give to them. But these necks were made in steel sections, something like a goose-necked lamp, and when they squeezed, they squeezed hard.

The coil went first around the backs of my calves, then my midsection, and finally and very quickly it began to wrap around my head. I pushed it up with my hands just in time to prevent it from crushing my windpipe.

Their tryst took but a few seconds, then they separated, leaving me gasping. I hung on trying to get my breath, but there wasn't time.

I'd stuck the sword in my belt before starting to climb, and with the two necks finally disengaged, I stabbed Hugo into the soft area behind the jaw and pulled myself up on a level with the head. Then I held on tight, pulled the sword out of my pants, and sunk a third of it into the mouth.

The rate of sputtering increased from an occasional spark to a continuous blaze.

During this time the still-working heads attacked without mercy. Fangs whizzed by my ears and neck. My coat was in shreds and a warm rivulet ran down my back. Fortunately, I was nested in a cluster of disfunctional heads and difficult for these three still-enterprising ones to get at. There was one, however, whose angle was a little better than the others and who had persistently done more damage. I turned my attention to him.

I moved to one side, holding the samurai blade between me and my attacker. Two thirds of it were exposed. Then I placed my head near the bare steel, daring it to strike. It did, missing me, but neatly wrapping its jaws around the sword.

No sooner had it made contact than sparks began to fly. Beneath me the entire structure stiffened. I could almost feel the electricity channeling down the wrong wires, blowing out circuit boards, frying switches, blasting fuses. The necks stopped moving. The hissing of the other two heads stopped and they froze.

The sun in the ceiling grew dim, then blinked out altogether. In a few seconds it came back on. Minamoto had had to switch to emergency power.

Fourteen

I pulled Hugo out of the soft plastic scales and let myself down. Now that it was still, the dragon didn't look so imposing. Just a big grotesque sculpture in plastic and steel in a ridiculous posture, biting its own head.

I took off my cashmere jacket. It had been ruined in the final skirmish. A slice had been opened in the back from shoulder to shoulder by one of the fangs. My back was also cut, but that would heal.

I was standing there examining myself for any other damage, when I heard a click like a casette tape being shoved into a player. Then a voice started speaking in academically clear English.

"In the time before there was time, before Amaterasu, Goddess of the Sun, had willed her grandson the islands of Japan and before his grandson, Jimmu, became the first mortal to ascend to the throne, Susano-o, the Impetuous Male, son of Izanagi, and Izanami, was traveling in the province of Izumo.

"There dwelled a great dragon. Eight heads sprouted from its many necks, and its eight tails filled eight mountain valleys. The dragon feasted on mortal flesh and ravaged the maidens of Izumo.

"The oppressed people of the province, hearing that a great warrior was in their midst, beseeched Susano-o to slay the dragon. Susano-o thought it a challange befitting a god.

"He chose the most beautiful maiden in Izumo as bait, and with his father's sword and a great many casks of *sake*, lay in wait for the beast with the eight heads and whose tails filled eight mountain valleys.

"The body of the beast was very vast and Susano-o heard it coming days in advance. The earth trembled and the sky became turgid with black clouds. Susano-o poured the wine into a trough and tied the maiden to a stake.

"The fierce dragon soon came, sniffed the *sake*. Overwhelmed with the novelty of the liquor, he drank his fill, and fell into a deep sleep.

"Susano-o stole from his hiding place and cut the maiden loose, telling her to go back to her village. Then, his father's sword in hand, he struck off each of the monster's heads.

"Not satisfied that by beheading it he'd killed it, he decimated the body one section at a time. So large was the dragon, this task took a hundred days.

"For twenty days he slew the necks and cut them to pieces. Then he proceeded down the back, upon which forests grew. This work occupied him another thirty days. Finally, he reached the base of the huge tail, so vast that clouds had gathered on it. He set to work hewing it apart, when his sword, venerable and mighty though it was, succumbed to the enormity of his effort, and the blade turned.

''But that day Fortune smiled down on Susano-o and he found another sword embedded in the dragon's tail. Quickly he finished his work, and when he was done, gave his newly-found sword to his sister, Amateratsu, the Goddess of the Sun. Because of where he'd found it, he called it 'Cloud-Cluster Sword.' ''

This recitation took two, maybe three, minutes and made about as much sense as anything had since I'd begun this assignment. As soon as the voice stopped and the tape clicked off, a panel opened in the wall to my left. I waited for more than thirty seconds, to see what would come through. When nothing did, I dropped what was left of my jacket, and walked over.

Through the door was a room modeled in the same stage-set fashion as the locale of my dragon battle. Instead of the wild blue yonder, the theme now was the mountains of Japan.

Murals of mountain scenery painted on the walls gave the illusion of being outdoors, an effect heightened by indirect florescent lighting from the floor. The decorations consisted of phony rocks and trees—papier-mâché and cloth from the look of them—painted to resemble the real thing. Through all this ran a mountain path and bisecting the path was a real mountain stream which flowed out of one wall across the room and disappeared. Over the stream was a sturdy-looking wooden footbridge which took up a good portion of the room.

I had learned by this time not to wonder overly much at anything I encountered here. I entered and examined the opening where the stream flowed out of the wall. I knew there was more to this house than I had seen, and I was anxious to find some way out of this series of rooms. Here I was subject to whatever mechanical torture Minamoto's whimsy could invent.

Unfortunately, the slit where the water entered was too narrow to allow me to escape. I checked to see if it could be widened, but it was concrete. Then I tasted the water. Salty. Apparently, it was being pumped in from the Mediterranean.

"That water's not for drinking, Mr. Carter," said a quiet voice just behind me. A heavy-set Japanese man dressed in the cowl and robe of a Buddhist monk was standing in the artificial foliage only a few feet from me. "I didn't mean to frighten you. I only wanted to say that if you need something to revive your spirit, tea will be served momentarily."

"I want to see Yoshitsune Minamoto and I want to see him now," I said, standing up.

"And so you shall. But you can't be presented to the Master dressed such as this. Here, put this on." Draped over his arm was a dark maroon robe. He held it out for me to take, but I backed away.

"You must trust me. You are a brave warrior. You defeated a machine it took the Master many years to build. We thought it was invincible, but you proved us wrong."

"You were watching?"

"We all watched. You were magnificent. Quite magnificent. You are a warrior of the first rank, and you will be treated here with the respect you deserve."

"Then if it's all the same to you, I prefer to keep the clothes I have on. No matter how torn they are."

"As you wish." He hung the robe on a tree branch as though to say if it were nothing to me, it was a rag to him as well. Then he turned to me with a polite smile. "We may go now. The Master is waiting."

He stepped aside to allow me to pass him on the path, but I motioned for him to go ahead. "You first," I said. He bowed and walked on in front of me. I followed.

We were halfway across the bridge when I stopped to ask a question. "What *is* all this?" I said, sweeping my arm to include the room as a whole. "And that other place, too. What are these interiors supposed to represent with their cotton clouds and phony flowers and trees?"

As I looked around, I noticed the door I'd come in had been shut. "What the hell's going on here?" I demanded. "Is this another trap?"

The monk didn't reply. His eyes narrowed. He stepped back a pace and threw open his robe. Underneath he wore a full outfitting of samurai armor: breast plate, skirt, and leggings, and on his hip was a samurai sword.

"Aaaayiii!" he yelled, drawing the sword and taking a swing at me. I dodged out of the way and he split a balustrade in the bridge railing. Then he reared back to swing at me again.

I didn't have a weapon, realizing Hugo was no match for the sword and not being sure I wanted to give his presence away just yet.

The monk let fly with the sword again and stuck it in one of the wooden crossbeams. While he was jerking it back and forth trying to get it free, I put some distance between us.

As I ran off the footbridge, I saw a long spear-like knife leaning against one of the supports. I was sure it hadn't been there a minute ago.

I picked up the spear and swung it in the air a couple of times to get the feel of it. Known as a *naginata,* or pole sword, it consisted of five feet of thick staff with two feet of vicious blade stuck in the end. I'd seen them in museums on visits to Japan, but never actually held one.

I didn't get much chance to practice. He was on me in

a few seconds, lunging and swinging the sword overhead in an effort to slice me in half.

I stopped the blow with the business end of the *naginata*. The two blades clanged together and the vibration stung my hands. Then I spun the weapon around and caught him on the side of the head with the staff.

It was a pretty neat move. I thought I'd clouted him good. I expected it to at least stagger him, but he never flinched. He came right back with two more sweeps of his sword. I caught one on the blade, but the second cut a big chip of wood out of the staff, and I realized I was going to have to be careful or I was going to end up with a short knife and a long useless pole.

As it was, I had something of an advantage. The *naginata* was about seven feet long overall, which if I could extend to its full length would put me out of range of the monk's sword.

But to use this advantage, I had to get inside his defenses. As long as he was on the attack and kept me fielding blows, the awkwardness of the oversized weapon worked in his favor.

He lunged at me with another overhand stroke. I caught it on the blade, but before I could turn and swing at him, he swung again, this time laterally, forcing me to move the *naginata* awkwardly to block it.

By this time we'd moved down the path away from the bridge. I let him have another blow, then I moved under and around behind him. There wasn't time to strike him from here before he'd turned to face me again. He was too fast and too good with his sword. But I was leading him back toward the bridge and that, I had calculated, was in my favor.

The bridge was arched and the man who stood on it was on a level a foot or two higher than his opponent.

Not much of a consideration when men fight with guns, but in swordplay there's a world of difference between striking up at or down to your adversary.

I felt the bridge planking under my feet. He swung and missed me. This infuriated him and he swung again with all his might. This time I stepped back and the blade stuck in the bridge. As he wrestled with it, trying to get it out, I laid the knife of the *naginata* on his shoulder, resting the cutting edge against his neck.

"Don't move," I told him, "or I'll flick your head off like a cigarette ash."

His eyes narrowed again and I pushed the blade a little closer to home.

"Which way is Minamoto?"

He nodded in the direction of the other side of the stream. I reached down and pulled the sword out, then flung it over the railing. It landed with a splash near where the stream flowed out of the wall. I spun him around and held the cutting edge at the nape of his neck.

"March."

We moved to the middle of the bridge. Then suddenly he leaped away from me and turned around.

"I am Benkei!" he shouted. "I am the monk of Enryaku-ji. Born a man with hair and teeth, I could lift a horse onto either shoulder and still slay a hundred men. It was I who stole the great bell of Mii-dera and carried it home on my back. And it was I who took the fore at the battle of Uji and who split in mid-air the thousand arrows of the Taira with my sword. Now in my old age I have fallen to a lesser man."

When he finished, he jumped over the railing into the stream.

I assumed he was going to retrieve his sword. I rushed to the railing with the *naginata* drawn back prepared to send it through the back plate of his armor on the fly if need be, but the sight that greeted my eyes from the stream below stopped me cold. Face down between the rocks, being washed over by the swift running water, his body bubbled and spit like a drowned radio.

I hurried to the foot of the bridge, then down the bank to the edge of the stream. His head was still popping and spitting blue sparks. I rolled him over with the staff of the *naginata*. He'd fallen face-first on a rock, smashing out all the features. But behind them wasn't blood and sinew, it was a tangle of wires, diodes and microprocessors.

"A robot!" I exclaimed.

"Not exactly, Mr. Carter," said a quiet voice from the bridge. Yoshitsune Minamoto looked down at me from above, his elbows resting casually on the railing. " 'Robot' is an out-moded term. Even 'automaton' hardly catches the elegance, the scientific sophistication of my creations."

"I don't believe it," I said, looking down at the inert form of the monk outstretched in the water. Only minutes before he had been a living, breathing man.

"Amazingly lifelike, isn't it? But you haven't come all this way and gone through this travail to gawk at useless machinery. Come."

He stretched out his arm and beckoned me. "Come," he said. "You have nothing to fear. Old Benkei was right in one respect. If there's anything that gains admiration here, it's prowess in battle. Come. You've certainly proven yourself."

I walked around to the foot of the bridge. He met me and took my arm.

"Where are you taking me?" I asked.

"Somewhere you can rest for a few minutes. Where we can talk."

"Talk about what?"

"What all this has been about," he said, making an expansive gesture with his hand. "Isn't that what you want to know?"

"You're a maniac," I said quietly. It was meant as a simple statement of fact.

"People have said that. It doesn't mean I'm illogical." He smiled, a grotesque expression that wrinkled skin all the way to the top of his bald pate, except for the smooth discolored areas around his temples. "Come with me," he said.

Fifteen

He led me across the bridge to the other side of the room, then down the path to a panel in the wall that slid open as we approached. Through the panel was a room even more massive than the one we'd just left and decorated in the same sort of way. Only instead of a stream there was a reflecting pool. Around the pool and throughout the room were an abundance of green plants, real ones, arranged in a lush garden. And above the pool, nestled in the shrubbery, was a wooden cubicle structure that I recognized immediately—a Japanese tea house.

"This is my retreat," he said with a hint of pride. "A man needs a place to meditate, no?"

"Some retreat," I said.

Just inside the room set against the wall were four locker doors. Minamoto pulled the first of these open and drew out a maroon robe identical to the one the monk had been carrying.

"My robot, as you called it, offered this to you and you refused to wear it. Won't you accept it now from me? You don't want to continue wearing those rags.''

"I'll keep the rags, thanks. And I want you to know I don't appreciate your gracious host routine.''

He replaced the robe in the locker and closed the door. "It is not a routine, as you say. I assure you, it is quite sincere.'' He pulled open the next locker and took out a black kimono.

"Then you'll have to excuse me, but I don't feel like being polite. When I come visiting, I don't enjoy being pitted against mechanical puppets for the entertainment of the host.''

He took off the jacket of his suit and hung it in the locker. Then he slipped on the kimono over his shirt and tie. "I can understand how you must feel. As a guest you have been treated disgracefully thus far. Please accept my apologies and allow me to assure you there are good reasons for the ordeals you've had to endure.''

He studied his image in a small mirror set on the inside of the locker door and adjusted the knot of his tie. Then he closed the locker.

"I would like to make this up to you in some small way by offering you a cup of tea and explaining. . . .'' He reached out to take hold of my arm, but I yanked it away.

"You're not sorry enough,'' I said. "It isn't just me. You compromised the security of an agency of the government of the United States *and* you exposed the entire population of the world to one of the most dangerous microbes in the history of germ warfare.''

He looked up at me rather amused. "What will you do? Arrest me? You forget where you are, Mr. Carter. The environs here are controlled by me. I am the law, the only law, within these walls.''

"I've seen your law and how you enforce it. I'm not impressed.''

His amused look faded. "Very well, Mr. Carter," he sighed, "do as you wish. Let me just say that anger becomes no man. Please don't tarnish my estimation of your prowess as a man of battle with a display of lack of self-control. I've brought you here at great trouble and expense to make a gesture to you of my esteem. I am going to retire to the tea house for a cup of tea. I would very much like to have you join me. Or you may remain here if you wish. When I return, we can make arrangements for returning you to your car and a safe trip back to Monte Carlo." He bowed, then stepped around me and walked off down the path in the direction of the tea house.

As soon as he disappeared into the trees, I went back to the wall panel. It was fastened tight with some kind of spring mechanism. I wedged the knife end of the *naginata* into the crack and pushed. Just as I was making headway, the tip of the blade snapped off under the pressure. I threw down the weapon in disgust and began feeling the door frame for a photo-electric trigger. It was then I noticed the unobtrusive black camera box hinged high in the ceiling and rotating with every move I made. The watchful eye of the computer, I thought. No wonder it wouldn't open.

It looked as though I was a prisoner here until Minamoto decided to let me out. I walked back to where Minamoto had changed his clothes. To one side was an arch fashioned with rough wooden beams and roofed with tree limbs and vines interwoven into a thatch. Beneath it was a small stone bench. I sat down for a minute to rest. It felt as though I'd been fighting this house forever.

Minamoto was right about one thing. I was burning with questions about him and this place and running off at the mouth wasn't going to get them answered. Chief among those questions were the particulars of how that monk Benkei was constructed. I had never seen the like of it. I had spent over fifteen minutes with it and never once suspected it wasn't real. An astounding achievement of bionic science. I had to have a better look at it and I was sure there were people in Washington who'd like to have a look at it, too. When I left this place, I was going to have to arrange to bring the monk's body with me.

Things were quiet down in the tea house, I thought, looking down in that direction. "A gesture of my esteem." I wondered what he'd meant by that. He thought I was something special because I'd learned to take care of myself.

I sighed and stood up. I figured enough time had elapsed to register my indignation. There was no shame now in going down and finding out what this was all about.

I considered fetching the robe Minamoto had offered me earlier, but then I thought this would be too much of a capitulation and I went as I was, Wilhelmina strapped in her holster around my chest, my shirt in tatters.

The path to the tea house is traditionally a series of stepping stones, some of which have certain rituals attached to them. One of these is the Water Basin, a stone urn set on a pedestal where the guest washes off the grime of the everyday world in preparation for the rarified atmosphere of the tea house. I dispensed with this. I had every intention of keeping the everyday world firmly in mind.

I went quickly up the wooden steps to the small opening in the wall known as the Wriggling-In-Place. I was supposed to take off my shoes, but I didn't. I wanted to show Minamoto that although I was coming, I was coming on my own terms.

I went in the only way I could, on all fours. In Japanese tradition one is humbled from the outset. Minamoto was busy preparing the tea. A small fire crackled beneath an earthenware pot and on the mat in front of him were a number of utensils and two ancient-looking cups.

When he saw me, he carefully laid the implement in his hand to rest, stood and made a deep bow. "Welcome," he said. "My humble tea house radiates with your presence."

I bowed in return, and when I did, I was sure he saw my shoes. If he was insulted, however, I couldn't tell it from his face.

I sat across the mat from him on my knees in a posture identical to his, and folded my hands in my lap. This seemed to please him, and when I was settled, he set about making the tea.

He removed the lid from the boiling pot and placed it on a small block of wood seemingly designed for just this purpose. Then he ladled a small amount of hot water into a bowl and used it to wash a wire tool. He then withdrew the tool and wiped it with a small napkin he kept folded neatly in his sash. When the tool was cleaned and dried, he carefully poured the dirty water into a third bowl. Every movement he made seemed to be part of a rehearsed ritual. All his concentration was required for the simplest operation.

He went on in this slow, precise way for ten minutes or more, ladling water, stirring in tea, each time wiping everything with his napkin, until at last he bowed and presented me with a cup containing a few ounces of thick, bright green tea.

I bowed and accepted it. Then I took a sip. It was terrible. Much too strong. I bowed again and put the cup on the mat.

I was about to murmur my thanks, when he indicated with a movement of his head that I mustn't talk. Then he picked up the cup I had used, took a sip, wiped the lip of it with one quick movement of his napkin, and returned the cup to the mat. Then he sat back on his heels with a pleased expression on his face.

And it was finished. Not much of a ceremony, I thought. And yet, something told me a lot hinged on these last few minutes. At least for Minamoto. Nothing was visible on his face, but his eyes and manner seemed to indicate deep emotions attatched to this simple little rite we'd just performed.

After a few seconds, he began the cleaning up. This step was every bit as complex and prescribed as the initial preparation. Every implement had to be carefully washed, dried, and laid out, and when that was done, each was separately carried behind a screen, until finally only the big water bowl remained. He took this out carrying it with both hands. Then he returned and knelt where he had been before and made me a low bow.

I bowed in response and this is the way we remained for the next several minutes, neither of us speaking. I listened to the sounds of the house around me. Each creak and thump was interesting. Outside, I thought, it must be close to dawn.

"Do you feel calmer now?" he asked at last. "More willing to talk?"

"Yes, I feel better. But that doesn't mean I'm still not angry."

"Anger held tightly in one's stomach and released in measured amounts can be a good thing."

"Is that what you brought me all this way and put me through this misery to tell me?"

"No."

"Then if you don't mind, I think you owe me an explanation . . ."

He held up a hand to stop me. "I will answer all your questions in good time, but please, let me tell the story in my own way."

"All right," I said. "Begin."

"We have a great deal in common, Mr. Carter," he began. "We are both warriors in a world that shuns war and persecutes those who practice it. And yet we both know the exhilaration of armed conflict and the marvelous finality of its resolutions."

"In what way are you a warrior?" I asked.

"I am samurai, the last of a great house of fighting men. I am named for one of the great heroes of Japanese history. Although I'm afraid my illustrious lineage doesn't mean much in the world today. Modern-day Japan is a long way from the Japan of my forefathers. We are a conquered people, Mr. Carter. When a nation is conquered, its past becomes suspect. Its people lose faith in their traditions. Believe me, Mr. Carter, it is not easy to watch a culture as grand as the one that flourished on our small islands for so many centuries die."

"I wasn't aware the culture of Japan was dying."

"It is. Westernisms creep in. The people grow soft. They forget the lessons of honor and devotion to duty their samurai forefathers taught them. When I was a younger man, I thought it was possible to wake the people out of their torpor. I thought that pointing out the signposts of danger would be enough to turn them around. But I was wrong. All it earned me was abuse and ridicule.

"My realization of the hopelessness of trying to save Japanese culture from extinction brought about one of the most difficult periods of my life. I was working for

Niji Electronics. I quit my job and went to live alone in the mountains. There I trained myself in the arts of self-defense, archery, swordsmanship. I became a samurai in fact, not just in name. In time they began to write newspaper articles about the crazy warrior living in the mountains and young men came to join me. A few at first, but gradually more and more. After a while, we became something of a political force in the government. Once again my hopes began to soar.

"But then legislation was passed prohibiting the forming of private armies and we were forced to disband. I tell you quite candidly, I was on the brink of despair."

"I don't understand what all this has to do with me," I said.

"Allow me to finish. The gods have taken mercy on me. Three months ago I was told I have cancer. It has entered the lymphatic system. I won't live out the year."

"Gigi didn't tell me . . . "

"Gigi doesn't know. She thinks I'm crazy, yet she loves me. She'll find out everything soon enough."

"I'm sorry that you're ill," I said, "But I don't know what I can do . . . "

"I have one last wish, a wish that you and you alone can fulfill. Will you come with me? There's something I'd like to show you."

He stood up. I stood as well, glad of getting the circulation back into my legs. Then he led me out the narrow entrance hole and down the garden path toward the reflecting pool.

"About ten years ago, I started monitoring the flow of classified information among the great Western governments," he began again as we walked along. "Mind you, my interest wasn't malicious. It's just that electronics and numbers have always come easily for me and deciphering the codes was such child's play. And I noticed your code designation, N3, kept cropping up time and again. I must confess, I became fascinated. I followed all your exploits. So when I began this last project of mine, you were naturally the man I thought of first."

We came to a bend in the path where the trees and bushes had overgrown their boundaries. We pushed the branches out of the way and I could see a small clearing up ahead.

"First," he went on, "I determined I needed a great deal of money, so I invented a system of winning at blackjack that is not only foolproof, it is undetectable. So I came here where I could win large sums and not have to pay taxes, bought this house and remodeled it. Then I set up a series of tests for you."

"Tests?"

"Yes. You are undeniably the greatest warrior in the Western world, but it remained to be seen if you were worthy of a samurai."

"Is that what all this has been about? Testing me?"

"Yes. Gigi contacted you first in Phoenix. Then it was my turn in Ann Arbor, and then here. Each test was designed to measure your mental and physical abilities under stress. I'm happy to say you passed admirably."

"Terrific." I still didn't know what all this was leading to. The clearing was just ahead of us, an empty space in the shrubbery about a hundred feet across, paved with fine white gravel.

"The only thing that remained was luring you out here. That's why I set up the ploy with the microprocessor as an inducement. I knew you really didn't need it. Once the codes were discovered broken, they would have to be changed in any event, but I thought as a challange it would appeal to your pride as a warrior, and I was right.''

I pulled away the leaves that hung in the entrance to the clearing and for the first time saw two stone benches set side by side at the far end. Against each leaned a suit of the hard leather armor similar in type to the one the monk had been wearing. There was also a samurai sword.

Sixteen

"Is this what you've been building up to all this time?" I asked, "a contest between you and me?"

"Yes," he said frankly. He moved past me onto the gravel.

"But that's absurd! Wait a minute," I said, taking his arm. He turned to look at me, his expression blank as stone. "You're laboring under a misconception. I'm not a warrior, not in the sense you think. I have a job to do, a dangerous job that requires me to learn how to take care of myself in some pretty tough situations. But that doesn't mean I enjoy killing. I don't do it for its own sake . . . "

He pulled away and continued walking toward the two stone benches.

"I can sympathize with your being sick," I said after him, "but I'm no executioner. If you want to commit suicide, you'll have to find somebody else to do the dirty work. Minamoto, are you listening to me? I'm telling you, I refuse to participate!"

He stopped walking and turned to me. "Don't you think I've anticipated that possibility?" he said quietly. "What makes you think I'd give you any choice?"

"What do you mean?"

"Surely you've noticed the mechanical functions of this house are controlled by a central computer. There are also dynamite charges in the footings of the foundation. Given the proper signal, the computer will set off the dynamite and the entire structure will topple into the sea. You have no alternative but to kill me and make sure that signal is never given."

He walked to the left-hand bench, sat down, and began strapping on one of the leather shin protectors. I came up and stood over him.

"What kind of signal?"

"A word. A code word. I've developed a predilection for codes. You must understand, I'm going to die one way or the other."

I sat down on the other bench and shook my head in disbelief. "Why don't you commit *hara-kiri* the way your forefathers did? Why drag me into it?"

"They had their battles, their chances for glory. This is mine."

"This is what you planned all along, isn't it? Find someone suitable and lure him out for a little duel to the death here in the garden. I could have been anybody, anybody at all."

"As long as you had the proper qualifications," he said, tying the last strap on the shin guard.

"I'm not going to let you use me like this," I said firmly. "You give the computer any signal you want, blow the house sky high, but I'm not going to be forced into fighting a battle, that is completely mad. And also, Minamoto, suppose I lose?"

He looked up and smiled broadly. It was the first

genuine smile I'd seen on his face since I'd met him.
"Then we'll meet in heaven," he said. He had strapped
on the one legging, gotten out the second, and was
fitting it around his shin. "Is this how you want to
die?" he asked. "In a fit of obstinacy? You have a
chance at survival . . . "

"What does it matter how I die? Once I'm dead,
that's it."

"Maybe that's the difference between our two cultures. You don't care how you die, so it doesn't matter
how you live."

I let out a sigh. There was no use in arguing with him.
"All right," I said. "But can't we dispense with the
armor? If we must fight, why prolong it?"

"Very well," he said, putting the one legging aside
and unstrapping the other, "no armor." He picked up
his sword and walked to the center of the arena.

I went over to where he was standing, carrying the
other sword in my hand. "I don't know if I have the
stomach for this," I said when I reached him.

He smiled, then drew back and swung at me with all
his might. I caught his sword on mine and fended it off
with a clang. "Now that it's you or me, it won't be your
stomach telling you what to do," he said.

He sprang back on his muscular legs and rushed me,
swinging like a woodsman. I backed up, blocking his
charge while pulling away from him. After fifteen or
twenty slashes, his momentum ran out and it was my
turn. I charged him, hacking and chopping for all I was
worth, backing him across the gravel.

A samurai sword is like that. It isn't meant for grace-
fully thrusting and running your victim through. It's
designed to hash a man to hamburger, and that's pretty
much what we must have looked like, a couple of
butchers going at it.

We charged and retreated, charged and retreated like this for thirty minutes without letting up. I was gushing sweat. It ran down my back, my arms, and into my eyes. He refused to lay back and let me kill him. He wanted to win.

Finally, at the end of one of my short flourishes, when I'd forced him back as far as I could, I pulled back for a second, panting. My hands were sweaty and the sword handle was slipping badly. And yet I had no more than rubbed my palms on the thighs of my pants and repositioned my fingers when he was on me again with a blow from overhead. Then came another and another. The man's stamina was unbelievable, I thought. How long could he keep charging me like this?

Minamoto smiled at my disbelief. It was the kind of smile you wanted to slice in half. I remembered the basement in Ann Arbor and how he'd kicked me in the ribs again and again. I knew now there'd been no reason for it. He was just being malicious.

He backed me across the arena, swinging from the right, from the left, overhead, left, left, overhead, overhead, overhead. I tried holding my sword stiffly in front of me and letting him hit at it while I looked for something to repeat itself in his stroke, something I could lay in wait for and exploit. But there wasn't anything, or my concentration wasn't acute enough to find it.

On top of everything else, I was running out of room. He had backed me against the wall of greenery that separated the arena from the reflecting pool below the tea house. He swung with all his strength, hoping even if he bounced it off my sword, the force of it and the bushes behind me would knock me off balance.

I parried, but I missed the pivot point of the blow. His sword slid down the flat side of my blade and sliced across my bicep.

Blood pumped out like a wellspring. We both stared at it. Crimson testimony to the mortality of this business we were engaged in. The sight of it dripping down my arm incensed me.

My anger over the high-handed way I had been manipulated into this situation, being asked to risk my life in something that was his affair and his affair alone, for no more reason than to placate his twisted vanity, suddenly boiled to the surface.

I began swinging like an enraged bull. I didn't care if I never landed a blow. If I couldn't cut him, I'd bludgeon him to death.

He back-pedaled, trying to get away from me, but I came after him on the run, swinging and slashing with everything I had. He counter-stroked each blow of mine (which was amazing considering how fast they were raining down on him) but my cuts were too strong. They popped his sword back into his face.

He knew he had to stay out from underneath me, which meant he couldn't stand and fight. He had to keep moving away or take the full force of what I was dealing him.

I had no intention of letting up. Now that I'd flushed him I knew I had to finish him off.

We vied around one full circumference of the arena with no change. I was still coming on strong, although I could feel myself weakening. It had been a long night and I'd already been through more than I cared to remember.

Finally, we reached the spot where he'd cut my arm. A bright red stain marked the gravel. Now I had him. I backed him into the shrubs, hacking at him like a madman. Like I'd gone crazy.

There was no place for him to go. I swung and swung, wearing him down. He kept trying to back up, but the bushes prevented him.

He fought valiantly on his tiny square of ground, but eventually I proved too much for him. He lost his balance and fell backward. I raised my sword for the *coup de grace*, but he somersaulted through the bushes back onto his feet again, knee-deep in the reflecting pool.

I didn't even think. I reached down and grabbed one of the florescent light fixtures which were wired in a loose series along the floor and threw it in.

He howled like an animal when the voltage hit him. The lights went black, except for a string in the ceiling that must have been on a different circuit. The water bubbled and he stood stock still, his eyes starting out of his head. He opened his mouth to scream again, but nothing came out. Just his cheek muscles shook. In a few seconds the sense was gone from behind his eyes. He'd gotten what he wanted. He was dead.

I picked up the fixture by the wire and pulled it out of the water. The body hesitated a moment, then the knees buckled and it fell into the water on its shoulder, the face submerged.

I waded in and rolled the body face up. The eyes still stared blankly and the mouth, frozen open, was partially filled with water.

I took a hold under the armpits and pulled him out onto the gravel. Then, laying him on his back, I used Hugo to cut the wet knot of the sash and the buttons off the shirt. Under the shirt was an undergarment of a material that did not cut easily when wet, so I quickly stripped off the kimono and the white outer shirt and pulled the undershirt up over his head.

It was then I noticed something peculiar about his arms. Each had a long thin scar that completely encircled it just below the shoulder joint. The scars were too neat and identical to have been the result of an accident.

He'd had surgery there, although I couldn't imagine why.

Right now, though, I was too preoccupied to wonder about it. I was looking for something else. I examined the front of the top half of the body and found it—in the flesh below the ribcage on the right side, a darkened square of skin.

The light was bad, the enormity of the room being lit by a handful of hundred-watt bulbs, but then the work didn't have to be cosmetic. Taking Hugo like a pencil, I stippled an incision down the side and across the front of the darkened area, until I'd made a long crimson "L" just above the muscle layer. Then I lifted the corner and took out a bloodied sack of surgical polyurethane. Inside was a hard lump.

I walked over to the pond and washed it off. Then I opened the sack with Hugo's razor edge, squeezed out the lump and laid it in the palm of my hand: a piece of computerized plastic no bigger than a dime.

I squinted at it in the light. There was no way of knowing if this was a copy or the real thing, and if genuine, if it had any value. But I'd come by it hard, fought through obstacle after obstacle to get it, and I wasn't about to leave it behind. This and something much more intangible—an affirmation of my faith in my own abilities.

I slipped the chip into the breast pocket of my shirt and buttoned it. Then I wiped Hugo against my trouser leg. I was about to put him back into his sheath when I noticed again the incisions that had been made on the upper arms. In the dim light the scars were the same ghostly noncolor as the tissue masses that bulged from either temple.

Could he have severed both arms, I wondered? Not likely.

I stooped down and began to do some more minor surgery. I cut a line along the scar on the left arm about half way around. Then I made another incision just like it six inches lower and connected them with a third cut down the soft underarm. Then I peeled back the skin. Underneath it looked like the insides of a sewing machine.

Bionic implants. So much for his amazing endurance. And so much for kicking myself for not being able to best him in Ann Arbor. In reality the man was an insufferable bully.

My curiosity piqued, I cut open one of the lumps on the side of the head. More circuitry, as I'd expected, and then something I didn't expect. Beneath a flap of skin, running from one temple around the back of the head to its twin on the opposite side was a fine steel wire insulated with plastic. An antenna, I thought. This meant he must have been in mental contact with his computer all the time, although I had no idea how he'd managed it.

Minamoto's superpowers thus laid bare, I stood up and put Hugo away. Then I walked over and picked up my sword, which I had left lying on the gravel, and carried it over to where its sheath still leaned with the suits of armor against the stone benches. I had decided to take it with me. Several days from now, when I had awakened from my long, well-deserved sleep, it would prove to me all this had been more than just a bad dream.

With the chip in my breast pocket and the sword in hand, I went back to the sliding panel, which as far as I could see was the only exit. It stood open. Apparently, now that Minamoto was dead, the computer saw no reason to keep me prisoner.

In the next room the lights were still on and water still

flowed in the stream. I walked down the path to the foot
of the bridge, then down the embankment to where I'd
left Benkei lying. Only he wasn't there.

Broken pieces of black plastic still lay on the rock
where he'd crushed his face and one of his sandals
dangled from the low-hanging rubber foliage down-
stream. But the robot was gone. I looked through the
shrubs on my side, then waded across and checked the
other. From the condition of the sand on the far bank a
heavy-set man in crepe-soled shoes had dragged something from the water, then picked it up and carried it.

I followed his footprints through the artificial bushes
and trees until they entered the path and I lost them.
Then I began searching the path on both sides to the
bridge and back again to see if at any point they left the
path.

This was very disconcerting. There was no telling
who had walked off with it. It could have been somebody connected with Minamoto, or some third party
who followed me in.

When I returned to my starting point after having
searched in both directions, it struck me that whoever it
was might still be in the room, watching and wondering
if he was going to have to kill me. I stopped walking and
listened. Below the bubbling of the stream water,
below even the hum of the air rushing in the ducts of the
ventilation system, there was a whirring sound, like the
spinning of a rotor in a small electrical device. It
sounded familiar. I'd heard it before, but I couldn't
remember where or when.

I went through the sliding panel into the room where
I'd fought the dragon. He was still there, big as a small
house, looking like a side-show freak with a sword
stuck in one mouth and another mouth biting it.

As soon as I came through the opening, I pressed my

back flat against the wall near the door and slowly drew out the sword. I held my breath and listened for movement in the other room. Nothing. Only the whirring sound that I still couldn't place. It seemed that now I'd identified it, I was hearing it everywhere.

I waited for several minutes, both hands ready on the sword hilt, but no one came. Finally, I rushed the door and stood in the empty opening, my gaze darting from corner to corner in the room I'd just left, but no one was in sight.

I untensed my muscles and let the sword fall. Maybe I was alone, I thought. Just me and the dragon, and that damned noise. Then I realized the sound was different here than it had been in the room with the stream. It was coming from a different direction. In fact, it was coming from the wall directly behind the dragon.

I walked over and laid my hand on the plaster from where it seemed to me the sound was originating. It was faint, but then the building was deathly quiet. I took out Hugo and began tapping, looking for hollow spaces. Two taps and I realized that what confronted me was not a wall at all, but plaster on fabric stretched over a frame. I cut through the fabric and peeled it back. Behind it was a niche and in the niche a movie camera whirred incessantly. It was set on a tripod and attached to a cable so it could be panned in any direction by remote control.

Then I remembered where I'd heard the sound of one of these cameras before. It was in the basement of the apartment house in Ann Arbor just before my initial contact with Minamoto.

I turned the camera around, unsnapped the rear compartment and pulled out the film casette. It was a Bashe, like the one I'd sent to the lab. I unbuttoned the flap of my breast pocket and was about to slip it in next to the microprocessor when something hard, about the consistency of a gun butt, hit the back of my head.

My knees failed and I fell to the floor. I rolled over and pulled myself onto all fours, staring at the floor boards, my head doing barrel rolls. I tried to get up, but another blow a few inches above my neck finished the job. I slumped and laid out face up, my head resting on the terrible hot place where I'd been hit. Then the pain, the light, the whirring noise—everything—ceased.

Seventeen

I came to the way I'd been trained to, letting consciousness flow into my body, giving no outward sign I was awake. I was stretched out on a narrow bed, my head throbbing like a bass drum.

With one eye I surveyed the room. Small with plain white walls and wood floor, with nothing in it but the bed I was on and a nondescript table. At the table in a rumpled white suit sat a man reading a newspaper. As he turned the page, he tipped his face in my direction. There was no mistaking that mug. It was Lo Sin.

Behind him was the door, a plain, solid-wood affair with a dead bolt lock. It was closed. He turned another page and I saw the blue-black barrel of a .38 revolver that lay on the table a few inches from his hand.

I rolled over and gave out a grunt.

"Good. You're awake," he said, casting a glance in my direction. He turned another page and held it between his plump fingers, perusing the back of it. "So, we meet again," he went on in that obnoxiously polite way of his. "Ordinarily, it might be pleasant finding a familiar face in these strange surroundings, but may I say that your face, Carter, is becoming most dreadfully tedious.''

I sat up and put my feet on the floor. ''How long have I been out?'' I asked, rubbing the back of my head.

''Several hours.''

I felt a lump under my hair the size of a baby's fist. It was going to be tender back there for quite a while.

''You were supposed to freeze to death,'' I said. ''What happened? You manage to convince those *Sherpas* that money was more important than some old monk's curse?''

''Let's just say I was able to persuade one of my guides that leaving a man in a mountain pass twenty thousand feet above sea-level without food or a tent for protection was a barbaric practice.''

''How much of your ill-gotten gold did it cost you?''

He didn't answer. I laughed even though it hurt. ''You were lucky.''

''We shall see what was luck, Mr. Carter,'' he said coldly, hunching over his newspaper again.

''So what's your angle this time?''

''Must you always suspect me?'' he asked, not looking up.

''Come off it. You wouldn't wish your own mother a happy birthday if there wasn't something in it for you. I should've known there was more to this than just some nut's attempt at suicide. Why'd you hit me anyway?''

''I didn't hit you.''

''Somebody did.''

''You were about to muck up some carefully laid plans.''

A soft tapping rattled the door. Lo Sin got up to answer it, keeping his front to me, the revolver in his hand.

Through the crack I saw a long-haired Chinese youth

standing in the hall. He looked like the kid I'd chased down the basement steps in Ann Arbor. On his feet, I noticed, were dirty, crepe-soled shoes. They spoke in Mandarin.

"Shall I bring it now?" asked the kid.

"Yes," said Lo Sin. "He's awake."

Then Lo Sin closed the door, and without looking at me sat back down, put the gun on the table and returned to his reading. There was the faintest play of a smile on his lips.

"You haven't told me why I got hit," I said.

"Carter, I don't mean to be uncivil," he said, putting down the paper and fixing a look on me, "but I clearly have the upper hand for once and you have no choice but to be patient." With that he turned back to his newspaper and ignored me, leaving me wondering.

Time passed. Two minutes, maybe three. Not long enough for me to figure a means of escape. Then another knock came at the door. This time he stood up and pointed the gun at me. "Get it," he said.

"Why? I'm sure it's for you."

"Don't be smart," he said, brandishing the gun between me and the door. "Answer it."

"Give me a minute." I got slowly to my feet. I hadn't been vertical for a while and I wasn't feeling very steady.

I leaned on the table for support. This brought me within a foot of his gun hand. I was about to make a grab for it when he moved back along the wall.

"Who is it you're so anxious to have me see?"

"Never mind. Just open it."

I put my hand on the knob, but I didn't turn it. I couldn't imagine what was on the other side. The Chinese kid with a pistol waiting to blow my head off?

"Go on," he coaxed. "It won't hurt you. Not yet, anyway."

I pulled the door open. At first I flinched, then I stared unable to believe my eyes. Standing nonchalantly in the doorway, his hands clasped calmly in front of him, was a man who looked exactly like me.

"May I come in?" he asked, smiling.

"Nick Carter, meet Nick Carter," Lo Sin hooted from behind me, obviously enjoying this joke.

I was too amazed to speak. He was perfect: same eyes, same cleft chin. He even had short whiskers growing where I sometimes have trouble shaving.

"Strains your credibility, does it, Carter?" laughed Lo Sin. "Your eyes bulging? I don't think I'd ever see the great Nick Carter so completely taken by surprise."

"Is he for real?" I asked, the words coming out of me in an awed whisper.

"Show him," Lo Sin demanded. The man opened his coat, which was identical to the one I'd been wearing earlier, and pulled his shirt out of his pants. Then he triggered a catch in his waist and a door swung open in his stomach. Behind the door was a battery pack.

"Actually," Lo Sin explained, "he's better than real. He doesn't eat. Just recharge him every other day and he's as good as new." This was grounds for another eruption of laughter. I sank onto the bed, staring dumbly. When he was through enjoying himself, Lo Sin harshly ordered the robot to sit down. The robot dutifully sat in a chair behind the table.

"It's uncanny," I said.

"Minamoto was a genius!" exclaimed Lo Sin. "Look at those eyes. Look into them. Would you ever believe he wasn't alive?"

The robot's eyes were a clear blue, like my own. Every hair, every crease was copied there, even a scar that had caused a small bald spot in my left brow. But I saw right away what Lo Sin was talking about. It wasn't the physical similarity. In the alteration of their size and the mercurial changes of the brows around them, the eyes seemed to be capable of the most subtle expression. As I stared, the robot blinked back at me with benign non-personality.

"What do you suppose he's worth?" asked Lo Sin excitedly. "A million? Ten million? Is there any limit to what you could ask for him?" He, too, stared at the robot, his narrow Oriental eyes wide with greed.

The room seemed to have been divided down an imaginary line: Lo Sin and I on one side, gawking with wonder and fascination at the robot on the other.

"Tell him who you are and who made you," Lo Sin demanded, waving the gun at the robot.

The machine smiled politely, an expression so like my own, it made me wince. "The Master created me after ten years of effort, begun in the late months of 1971 and only just now finished. I was the second unit of a group of twenty, eighteen of which remain uncompleted. I was constructed as a gift for Master Lo Sin and I am programmed to follow any order he gives me. When he sells me as he plans, I will be reprogrammed to follow the orders of whomever Master Lo Sin choses."

I turned to look at Lo Sin. "He's grotesque," I said. "You don't actually think you're going to fool anybody with this . . . this puppet, do you?"

The big Chinaman moved around in front of me and sat his heavy frame down draping one hip over the edge of the table. The gun rested casually against the crease where his trousers pulled tautly across his thigh.

"Of course, I will, dear boy. Not forever, perhaps, but for a while. Long enough. Think of him not as a robot, but as a guided missile, able to gain access to places where only you and you alone can go. Always armed to the teeth, but acting on the orders of whoever programs him."

"You mean Washington?"

"It's a possibility. Mind you, it would take a good deal of money to get me to part with him, but there are those who would pay dearly to see certain friends of yours eliminated."

I thought of the casual way I often walked into Hawk's office, the way he sometimes stood gazing out the window when he greeted me.

"And this was your brainchild," I said grimly, "ten years in the making."

"That's right. I met Minamoto ten years ago, when he was living like a Spartan in the mountains above Osaka. His army had been taken away from him. He was on the verge of throwing himself into the sea. I'd heard of him through my usual sources and you know my penchant for things out of the ordinary. When I found him, he was everything I'd been told he was and more. When I saw Benkei waiting on him hand and foot and realized he was bionic and not human, I knew I'd discovered a gold mine. Why a character out of Japanese folklore? I asked myself. Why not a real man?

"Minamoto pointed out the difficulties involved and we hit on this plan to iron them out, whereby he'd get what he wanted and I'd get what I wanted. You see, in order to program a bionic replica indistinguishable from the real thing, precise measurements have to be taken. Movements have to be broken down into their components, nervous habits have to be carefully blue-printed. The voice, every aspect of a man's physical presence has to be minutely duplicated. It is an enormous job. Fortunately, the romance of dying like an ancient samurai and doing his bit to undermine the 'stranglehold of the West,' as he called it, appealed to Minamoto, and he was more than happy to go along with what I had in mind.

"So you see, every move you made here and in Ann

Arbor was carefully monitored with cameras and other devices. Then the information was analyzed and broken down in the computer. Once we had the machine, it had to be properly programmed to act like you.''

The robot sat listening to the story of his creation with a bland, passive smile.

''And I messed things up when I found the camera,'' I said.

''You severed a critical link in the plan. There was a lapse of three weeks from the time we took the information to the time the programming would be complete. This was made doubly difficult in that we had to do it without Minamoto's help. Which meant we weren't going to make the switch here at the castle. There was an accident planned. A munitions truck in Riyadh would inexplicably explode. You wouldn't survive, but our friend here would. But it was essential you left tonight thinking this affair was over and done with. When you found the camera and took the film, you left us no choice . . . ''

''I see. And now that you've told me all this, you're equally obliged to . . . ''

''Precisely.'' Lo Sin smiled and let the heft of the gun bounce against his thigh. ''We'll have to speed up the programming, but I've been informed this won't present any insurmountable problem.''

''And you intend to just blast me in the head with that cannon? As artfully as all that? After all this time, can't you come up with something more inventive?''

A grin spread slowly across Lo Sin's face, a horrible grin that split his lips away from two rows of bad teeth and gathered fat from his cheeks and jowls before it was completed. ''As a matter of fact, a rather novel idea has occurred to me,'' he said. ''Your expression when you opened that door and saw your own face staring back at you so tickled me . . . honestly, Carter, I haven't had a good belly-laugh like that in years . . . that I've decided to let our friend pull the trigger. I think it should be highly amusing to see you killed by your own hand.''

I'd figured something like this. It was just the kind of macabre twist that would appeal to Lo Sin. But it had dawned on me, too, that between them there was only one weapon, which meant at some point Lo Sin was going to have to hand the gun to the robot. At the time of transfer they would be vulnerable, because it is impossible to hand someone a gun and aim it at the same time.

I had been watching his movements with the gun for the last several minutes. Everytime he waved it around my heart jumped. I poured every thought into obtaining that weapon. I wanted it. My survival depended on it.

Lo Sin stood and turned to walk around behind the table, taking the gun from his right hand and putting it in his left, talking all the while: ''So, my young friend,'' he said, referring to the robot, ''the time is at hand for you to come of age.''

So saying, he moved behind the chair until he was standing behind and above the still-seated machine. He held the gun in front of the robot's face with the left hand so it could grab it with its right, still pointed at me.

The robot sat listening to what Lo Sin was saying, his eyes focusing first on the gun, then on me. Then he reached out his hand to take hold of the butt, all this happening in a split-second's time.

It was the moment of truth, now or never. I lashed out with my right foot to kick the table into their faces and occupy them while I charged, hopefully to gain control of a gun that would be up for grabs.

My foot hit the table, but the table didn't moved. There was a thud when the legs of it lifted an inch or so then snapped back to the floor. I looked to see what had happened and the robot was smiling at me, both hands flat on the table top and a portion of his weight holding it down.

Lo Sin was grinning from ear to ear. ''I should have warned you, Carter. He knows all your tricks and can anticipate your every move. He's also stronger, faster. In a way, he's a kind of a super-you.''

Let him anticipate this, I thought, and dived for the floor coming up with the table on my back. The gun discharged. The powder burned all the way down my spine as the slug ripped into the mattress behind me. I grabbed the bottom of the table in both hands and pushed it up, throwing the two of them against the wall. Lo Sin got the worst of it. The robot was somewhat protected by his bulk.

''Carter!'' Lo Sin shouted, his voice strained by the fact his face was being squeezed against the wall. ''Give it up! This is hopeless!''

Lo Sin had been standing when I hit him with the table, so I had the top half of his body and both his arms pinned. But the robot had been sitting, and although I knocked the chair over, only his shoulders and head were caught. I fully expected him to slip out the side of my makeshift vice. This didn't worry me. He wasn't armed. It was Lo Sin with the gun who was the problem and I had all my weight holding him at bay.

But the robot didn't slip out. He reached out from under the table top and smacked the underside with the side of his hand.

I wondered what he was up to. But I'd no more than gotten the thought in my head, than he'd hit it again and splinters of wood started flying. One more hit and I saw a perfectly good oak table being laid to waste. The time had come, I decided, to make a hasty retreat.

I dropped the table and made a rush for the door, but the robot's legs, which were splayed out in a ''v,'' tripped me up and I overshot it. I regained my balance against the wall, only by this time the robot, with incredible agility, had pulled himself to his feet.

There wasn't time to be fancy. I put my arms out in front of me to push him out of the way. He swept my arms aside and reared back for a haymaker aimed at my jaw that, combined with the speed my head was moving toward it, would have broken my jaw and cheekbone, too.

Luckily, I ducked and it glanced off my head, and while it didn't feel great, it didn't do the damage he thought it was going to.

When he missed, it threw him off balance to the outside. I kept coming and my momentum pushed him a little further in that direction, right into Lo Sin, who was still trying to collect himself after his ordeal with the wall and having had a table dropped on the tops of his feet. They collided and while they were trying to untangle themselves, I threw open the door and dashed out into the hall.

"Carter! I'll kill you!" Lo Sin's voice reverberated down the corridor. A shot boomed and the bullet split wood in the support beam a few feet ahead of me.

I ran around the corner and saw two figures hurrying down the hall in my direction, the Chinese kid and another Oriental in a white lab coat. I ducked back and flattened myself against the wall. They hastened around the corner, half-running in response to Lo Sin's shouts and the gun shot they'd heard. I held my breath and they went right past me. Then I slipped around and headed up the hall in the direction from which they'd come.

Eighteen

I ran for fifteen minutes without a rest, down halls and up stairs, checking over my shoulder every few seconds to make sure Lo Sin and his crew weren't gaining on me.

I was no longer in the part of the house where I'd drunk tea and fought with Minamoto. I'd vaulted across a courtyard a few minutes ago and entered the castle tower, or "keep," as it's called in Japan.

Things here were radically different. The halls were low-ceilinged, wide, and unlit, and the walls, what there were of them, were rice paper panels, the type the Japanese traditionally use to divide their houses. But for the most part, there were no walls, just railings of roughly-hewn wood strung between support beams enclosing large empty spaces.

It was this way floor after floor. I was getting higher and higher in this part of the house and there didn't seem to be any change. Whenever I stopped to listen, I heard them on the floor below. And I was fast running out of stairs to climb.

Finally, from a long, deserted hall, dark because it was on the moonless side of the house, I turned the corner into another hall, this one lit by a long window through which the moon beamed. I stopped running when I got to the window and stood holding on to the sill, panting. I needed a moment to catch my breath.

The way I saw it, I had two choices: get out and get help or stay and try to figure out a way to detonate the dynamite charges in the foundation footings, the ones Minamoto had talked about shortly before he died.

If I got out, I doubted I'd make it back before they'd all fled, equipment and everything, which meant there was a possibility I might lose track of my bionic duplicate. Under no circumstances could I allow that to happen.

On the other hand, those dynamite charges had been weighing on my mind since I'd first heard about them. With the simple flip of a switch, I could destroy the house and everything in it. There was something in the neatness of that that appealed to me. The trick came in finding the switch and figuring out a way to flip it. That was, provided Minamoto wasn't just blowing out hot air when he threatened me.

I heard their footfalls thudding in the hallway behind me and took off again. I hung a right down a hall lined with a bank of windows all casting a square of moonlight on the floor, then another right into one that was dark. Soon, I knew I should come to a staircase that would take me to the next level. I realized that by this time there couldn't be too many levels left, but I thought there should be at least one more. The only problem was I'd already traversed three-fourths of the tower's perimeter and still hadn't seen any stairs. Then I came around a corner and saw something obscured by the shadows. I'd almost run right past it.

As a staircase, it was much narrower than the stairs on other levels. There four men might have past abreast. Here there was barely room for me.

At the top of the stairs was a locked door. I slammed it with my shoulder and it flew open. Inside the room was small and dark, but the outside walls were all window. It was apparent, though I couldn't see much, that it had been inhabited not too long ago. There was a desk in the middle of the floor and bookcases against one wall.

I didn't have time to examine any of this, however. I heard them coming on the floor below, and I had to find a place to hide, quickly.

There was no glass in the window, just a broad shutter hinged at the top and held open by several long-necked hooks fastened to the eaves outside. I reached out and pulled down hard on the shutter. The hinges creaked from disuse, but it felt solid. I stood up in the window, got a good grip on the shutter's frame, and stepped out into empty space. For a second I dangled at the end of the shutter like a water drop at the end of a wet knife-blade, a cold wind whipping the shirt against my back. Two hundred feet below me, craggy rocks waited like gnarled teeth.

I turned myself around and worked my way down hand over hand to where one of the iron hooks held the shutter open. I latched on to the bottom of it with one hand and got the other hand around it a few inches higher. Then I heard the sickening sound of metal wrenching out of wood.

I looked up and my stomach sank when I saw an inch of the hook's threading had been torn from its anchor. My weight was too much for it.

My only hope was to redistribute my weight and take some of the burden off this one corner. Frantically, I began to pull up until I could get a leg over and a hand in the eaves. I put the tips of the fingers of my other hand into the crevice where the shutter was hinged and hauled myself onto the back of it, placing the sides of my shoes on a narrow strip of wood along the bottom.

I made it without a second to spare. I'd just managed to sidestep my way out to the middle to avoid it collapsing under me, when they burst into the room, Lo Sin, the duplicate, the Chinese kid, and three or four others. They turned on the light and began searching.

I was right. It was some kind of study, probably Minamoto's. They rummaged through the closets, pulled the bookcases from the wall, and looked under the desk. Then they shook their heads.

"The door's been forced. He must be in here," Lo Sin said in gruff Chinese. "You wait and keep watch," he told the robot. "The rest of you come with me."

They hustled out and the robot sat down in the desk chair. I spied between my handholds on the crevice, anxious to see what he would do when left alone.

Thirty seconds passed. He sat bolt upright in the chair, staring forward. A minute, two minutes. He stirred not a muscle.

He was listening, I was sure of it. And his hearing was probably better than any human's. I wondered if he could pick out the rise and fall of my breathing through the hum of the wind and the sound of the surf splashing below us.

I didn't dare move. The least creak of the shutter's hinges might tip him off, and I didn't need more than one demonstration of his amazing strength to know I didn't want to tangle with him unless it was necessary. So we waited, like a mouse being stalked by a blind cat, until I heard a sound like metal straining. I looked down and saw the weakened hook about to pull loose.

I watched the robot anxiously, trying to determine if he had heard it, too. Then I watched the hook. It was pulling out, this time silently, a millimeter at a time. Another few seconds and it would give way. There was no telling if the other hook would hold if this one gave out, but my guess was it wouldn't—which meant in a short time I was going to be sliding off my perch and swan-diving two hundred feet to my death, unless I did something fast.

Lo Sin suddenly walked in the study door and motioned to the robot. ''Come with me,'' he said. ''He fooled us. He must have broken the door, then hid in the shadows when we came in. Quickly, we have no time to lose.''

The robot followed him out without a word, leaving the door open and the lights on.

They weren't gone more than a second, when the hook pulled free and the other snapped right after it. I plummeted off the rough wood and would have nose dived into the jagged rocks below, had I not managed to hold on to a thin strip of molding along the bottom of the shutter.

I hung by my fingertips, my heart beating in my mouth. Below in the moonlight the waves coiled and uncoiled on the rocks.

I had to act fast. My fingers weren't going to hold on forever. By bouncing myself against the side of the tower, I was able to pull the shutter far enough from the window to put my thumbs underneath. Then I slid my hands along the bottom of the frame, working my way back to the corner. This was an agonizing process. I reached my goal just as my fingers began to cramp.

The object I had in mind was a short strut which supported the gable that jutted out over the window. It was quite a bit below the window, but I figured if I could get my feet on it, at least I wouldn't be in danger of falling.

I got one foot in the V the strut made with the side of the building, but it was the wrong foot. It was the right, which left me plastered against the rough shingles with my hands hooked on the bottom of the shutter and one foot stretched way to one side. It was an impossible position.

With a little more maneuvering I managed to extend myself out even further on the shutter frame and hook my calf and eventually my knee into the strut. From there it was sheer strength alone that got me upright, straddling the strut, and looking down at the choppy surf of the Mediterranean.

I was still a long way from being out of this mess. I stood as best I could and reached for the window. The only problem now was the shutter. It hung down in front of the opening, and while I could get my hand on the sill, the shutter prevented me from swinging myself in. The only solution was to put one hand on the window and the other on the frame inside the shutter and just muscle my way up.

It was equivalent to an iron cross on the standing rings, but not impossible. I got a good grip, making sure my hands were dry, then heaved with all my strength. The muscles pulled taut, those in my arms and down both my sides.

I raised myself until the top of my head was level with the sill, but I needed to go further to where I could bend my body and pull my legs up.

I was close, but not quite there, when a familiar pain began to grow in my side. It was the point of contact where Minamoto had kicked me in Ann Arbor what seemed like eons ago. My body began to quiver. I was losing it. Suddenly I let go and fell back onto the strut, still holding the shutter in one hand and the sill in the other.

For a minute or more all I did was pant and lay with my feet dangling. My muscles felt as though somebody had tried to pull them out of their tendons. I looked down and watched the waves crash into the rocks below, like a mouth forever opening and closing. I knew I was going to have to try it again. It was just a matter of building up the momentum and strength.

Several minutes went by. I took a deep breath and stood up. This time, I told myself, I wasn't going to play it safe by keeping my feet on the strut until the last minute. It only hindered my balance. I was going to have to just dangle, and if I didn't make it, then the disaster would be complete.

I took hold again and stepped off the strut. Now it was just me and the window and two hundred feet of empty space. I pulled with everything I had, pushing the shutter out away from the window at the same time that I raised my head.

It was bearable this time. I was higher. I could see into the room. My whole body was shaking with the effort. I tucked into a pike position and threw both legs over at once.

I hit the floor rather awkwardly, half my body outside of the sill, the lower half in, but I was safe. I straightened up and looked around in the light.

The furnishings in the room fit with Minamoto's idea of himself as the warrior prince. Everything was cut down to the minimum, simple shelves, drafting table, chair, desk, reading lamp. It seemed odd that Lo Sin hadn't wrecked the place looking for me, but then I remembered at times he was capable of peculiar little acts of respect, like the way he must have deholstered Wilhelmina while I was unconscious, satisfied himself she was empty, then returned her. She'd been there when I woke up, riding under my arm just as always.

I went around to the desk and started rummaging through drawers. I needed a gun, and although chances were good Minamoto didn't even own such a thing, I had to give the place a once-over just to make sure.

The first drawer contained writing materials, pens, paper, paper clips, erasers. The second, more paper, investment brochures, keys of various kinds. I grabbed these and stuffed them in my pocket. They might come in handy if I ran into a lock I couldn't open.

The bottom drawer was more interesting. It was packed with newspaper clippings. I began looking through them and they read like an AXE scrapbook. Every article dealt with an assignment the agency had tackled over the last ten years. And in every case I'd played some part. It was all there in detail.

So Minamoto'd done his homework. I threw the clippings back in a heap and slammed the drawer. Then I pulled the chair aside and opened the thin middle drawer just under the desk top. I'd skipped this one because I thought it was too narrow for a revolver.

There was nothing inside but an old book, placed squarely in the center of the drawer, and so obviously and deliberately situated in that spot, that I thought for sure it was booby-trapped.

I carefully flipped over the front cover. It was a copy of the *haiku-sinatori*, an epic Japanese poem. It was for the samurai what *The Iliad* was for the Greeks. Then I realized how absurd it was to think this book was rigged with explosives. It was situated this way because of the special significance Minamoto placed on it.

I picked it up and began to leaf through it. I understand much of spoken Japanese, but I don't read its written characters easily without a dictionary. Most of it was unintelligible.

I came across one page, however, where Minamoto had drawn a pen line down the side of a column, the method of underlining Japanese. It was a passage concerning the repulsion of the Mongol invaders from Japanese shores in the thirteenth century. Roughly translated it read:

. . . And after beseeching Amaterasu (Goddess of the Sun), a cloud no bigger than the span of a man's hand appeared in the evening sky. It swelled and billowed until it blotted out the sun and cries of uneasiness were heard from across the water where the Mongol vessels lay anchored.

By nightfall a mighty storm rose up and the wind raged and beat at the waves like a maddened herdsman, crashing them against the Mongol hulls, driving their ships into the rocks and each other, and laying their sails flat upon the sea.

And in the dawning light, when the wind had subsided, the sea was seen to be strewn with wreckage as though *tegu* [a finely-chopped kindling wood used in the tea ceremony] had been scattered over the water.

Emperor Kameyama bent his knee in prayer to Amaterasu and called the wind *"kamaikaze"* or divine.

The character for *kamaikaze* was underlined twice. Interesting, I thought, from a cultural point of view, when one considered what the word meant to Americans who'd lived through World War II and remembered the dreaded *kamaikaze* pilots who threatened our Pacific fleet with their suicide dives into a ship's stacks or bridge. To the Japanese it meant a wind sent from heaven that saved their country from invasion.

Interesting . . . but it wasn't a gun. I threw the book back into the drawer and closed it.

There didn't seem to be much point in looking further. I was going to have to find the main computer and take my chances unarmed.

Nineteen

It wasn't until I got down to what I guessed to be the third level from the bottom that I bumped into the surprise Lo Sin had left there for me.

I had come down the six or seven floors from Minamoto's study as cautiously as I could, stepping as lightly as possible, being wary of every creaking floorboard, and it had taken me a good fifteen minutes.

After tiptoeing down a long, dark hall, keeping to the shadows to avoid a trapezoid of moonlight that lay on the floor, I suddenly saw the orange glow of a cigarette grow bright for a second, then go dim again.

I froze. The glow came from under the window less than twenty feet away. He was sitting on the floor, whoever he was. I could barely make him out in the shadow.

There was no way of telling if he'd heard me. I stayed like I was, still as a statue, not daring to breathe. The cigarette wavered back and forth, glowing bright again, then dimming.

Several minutes slipped by. Then he stood and leaned out the window, flicking the cigarette into the sea. Judging from his silhouette, he was young, French, and wearing a turtleneck sweater. Out from the shadow of his body extended the long muzzle of an automatic rifle.

Local muscle, I thought. One of Lo Sin's recruits.

I could have rushed him from where I was and shoved him out the window onto the rocks below. He'd be too surprised to put up any resistance, and chances were any outcry he made would be lost in the sound of the waves. I could do that, I thought, but it would cost me the rifle.

So I waited. He stared out the window for several minutes, mumbling something to himself. While he was preoccupied, I moved a step or two closer. Eventually, he tired of whatever he was thinking and sat back down. I was within six feet of him by this time and obviously he still hadn't seen me.

He spread his legs out on the floor, resting his back against the wall, the rifle across his lap. He pulled a pack of cigarettes out from underneath the sweater, lit one with a lighter, and put the lighter down next to him on the floor. He blew a billow of smoke into the moonlight, then leaned his head back against the wall, exposing his throat and the faint shadow of his Adam's apple.

I was close enough now. I raised my left foot into a kick position, then slammed it into his windpipe. His head bounced against the wall and he fell forward on the floor, writhing back and forth, holding his throat and barking like a seal.

This went on for thirty seconds. Finally I picked up the rifle and walked over to him, raising the butt of it and watching for an opportunity in his gyrating to bring it down on the back of his skull and put him out of his misery. But before I could, he stopped moving and just twitched. I checked his pulse. He was dead.

I rolled him over, pulled off the turtleneck sweater, and tried it on. It wasn't a great fit, but it would do. Then I shouldered the rifle and continued on down the stairs.

Two more waited for me outside the door. They were huddled together in the courtyard, lighting cigarettes by cupping their hands over a match.

"I don't see why we don't just set fire to it and smoke the American out," one said in French. He too was wearing a turtleneck, and carried his rifle by the barrel.

"He wouldn't like that," the other said.

"Sometimes we think too much of what *he* says."

I watched them from just inside the tower door. It was the way I'd come in and, as far as I knew, the only way out. I brought the rifle to my shoulder and fixed its sights on the head of the guard nearest me. But I didn't fire. It would have been a stupid move. I followed him for a few minutes with the gun trained on him, then put it down.

There had to be another way, less sloppy. I didn't want to raise an alarm, and I didn't want to take the chance of getting pinned down in a gun battle.

So I reached into my bag of tricks for an old one. I went back upstairs to where the other guard's body lay stretched out by the window. I lay the gun on the floor and felt the rough beams that acted as room dividers until I found a sizable loose chip of wood. Then, taking up the gun, I wedged the wood between the trigger and trigger guard, pulling the trigger back just short of the point where the gun would fire. Then I stood the weapon carefully in the corner.

Next, I went back to the body and got out the cigarette pack from the breast pocket of the dead man's shirt. I took one out and lit it. It tasted good, strong and French, and I hadn't had a cigarette in a long time. I drew another couple of puffs, then placed the cigarette on the wood chip so it would eventually burn through. Then I went back downstairs to wait.

It didn't take long. I'd just reached the bottom and gotten myself into position when the gun discharged and the recoil sent it clattering across the floor.

In a second the two guards charged the door, past me, and on up the stairs, their guns at the ready. When they were out of sight, I slipped out into the moonlit courtyard.

The outside area was paved with the same crushed whitestone as the courtyard I'd crossed when I first entered the main part of the house. In the moonlight it glowed like a light table. It was impossible to cross it unseen, but I did my best to be inconspicuous, running alongside the courtyard wall, keeping to the shadow.

When I got to the first building on the other side, I pulled myself up to the narrow window ledge and peeked in. The first room was an anteroom of some kind, with Lo Sin sitting in a corner of it, smoking. The ashtray by his arm was full to overflowing with cigarette butts and ashes.

Across from him, through a wall of glass panels, a group of what looked to be doctors were working in an operating theater. They had on gowns, gloves, and masks for their faces. Then I noticed a thick rubber seal over the door frame and I knew at once it wasn't an operating theater at all, but a dust-free room. I'd seen one before at NASA Research in Houston.

On the table in front of these men my replica lay stretched out, although the front of his face had been removed. Wires and different electronic components hung out onto the table. In the wall on a TV screen numbers and schematic drawings flickered back and forth. The technicians studied the monitor, worked, then studied some more.

I let myself down. This wasn't the building. The central computer was housed elsewhere.

The other low building had no windows and only one door. The door was solid steel and had a heavy lock in the doorknob. I tried it cautiously. It was secured.

I was about to slip a credit card between the door and the jamb, when I heard someone coming. I ducked into the narrow space between the low building and the main part of the house just in time to see a door in the courtyard wall open and a man in a white lab coat emerge carrying a tray of coffee and sandwiches. He walked past me to the door I'd just tried to open, produced a key from a long chain in his pocket, selected one and put it in the lock. Then he turned it and pulled the door open, and began awkwardly trying to get the key out.

I charged out from the shadows and grabbed him from behind. "Don't move," I told him in Japanese, holding Wilhelmina's cold but empty barrel to the back of his head. "And don't be nervous. Your friends inside wouldn't want you to spill dinner."

He gulped once audibly, then we shuffled in together. I closed the door behind us with my gun hand.

The three technicians working inside were too preoccupied to notice us at first. But eventually, one by one, they all looked up from what they were doing and their jaws dropped. I must have looked half crazy to them.

"Nobody moves and nobody gets hurt," I said.

They quickly nodded their understanding, then cleared out of the way as I forced the one I was holding into the chair behind the video display terminal.

"Get it so I can talk to it," I said.

He looked up at me blankly.

"Type in your access code."

He typed something rapidly, and a line of numbers appeared on the screen above the keyboard. Then the computer typed a line. *Good morning, Mr. Yashika.*

"Tell it you want to see the schematics for the dynamite implacements in the building foundation," I said.

He typed in the request. The computer figured for a split second, then replied, "Do you have the code word?"

Yashika and the others looked at me expectantly. I was afraid of this. Minamoto had said it was a verbal command. But I had the feeling it didn't have to be given verbally, because Lo Sin had no doubt planned to use the self-destruct mechanism to obliterate the evidence of what he'd done here. And by the time he'd gotten around to pushing the button, Minamoto would have long been dead. So there had to be manual access to the mechanism, that much I knew, but I'd hoped the information wouldn't be further blocked by another code. Looked like I was wrong.

I had to think and think fast. I could have Lo Sin called over here, then jump him when he walked in the door. But he knew that my gun was empty and I'd end up having to fight my way out of here and maybe losing.

I looked around the room. Tape disks spun back and forth behind Plexiglass doors; the control module lights blinked as the computer awaited my decision. The technicians all stared, beginning to suspect a weakness.

I had to come up with a word, any word. Suddenly I had it and I said, "*Kamai-kaze.*" Somehow I knew this was the right word, especially since Minamoto had underlined the passage that referred to it in the *Haiku-Sinatori*.

The luck was running my way. *Thank you*, the computer typed up on the screen, and in a second a cut-away view of the castle as it was situated on the rock cliff flashed on with arrows showing where the charges had been placed under and behind the building.

"Instruct it to detonate," I told Yashika.

His eyes widened with horror. "I can't do that. Everything will be destroyed."

"Then get out of that chair. I'll do it." I gave him a shove and he landed on the floor on his backside. One of the other technicians helped him up, the two of them looking at me as though I were foaming at the mouth.

I typed in: *Detonate charges. Order not to be countermanded.*

Within a few seconds a terrific roar welled up from the ground below us. The little building, even though it was made of cinder blocks, shook. One of the tape drives smashed face first onto the floor, scattering Plexiglass in all directions. The technicians held on to the furniture and looked at the ceiling and each other wide-eyed.

Outside, lumps of granite that had once been walls and cornice pieces and roof thundered to the ground. I gripped the sides of the console to keep my chair from rolling with the floor as it pitched seaward.

A crack opened in the wall just below the clock, beginning at the ceiling and running downward. Just before it made it all the way to the floor, the rumbling suddenly stopped. Everything was still.

Plaster dust filled the air so thick I could hardly see. The technicians and I all looked at one another wondering what was coming next. Then the door flew open and Lo Sin burst in, bringing with him a man in a white lab coat and two of his guards with automatic rifles.

"What's going on here?" he demanded. When he

saw me, his face became livid. "You! I thought you'd be dead by now, trying to escape."

"I didn't try to get out," I smiled. "Minamoto mentioned the dynamite before he died. I couldn't resist the opportunity to get rid of you and that bionic puppet of yours at the same time."

"Fool! Don't you realize what you almost did? . . ."

He was about to tell me when another of his soldiers ran into the room. His face was ash-white and he was out of breath. It was one of the men who had been guarding the tower.

"Everyone out!" he shouted in French. "No time to lose! It's falling into the sea, the whole rock face. We'll all be killed!"

The technicians didn't need a translation. Panic swept the room like a brush fire. They all made a run for the door.

"Halt!" screamed Lo Sin. His two guards pointed their guns and everybody stopped. "No one leaves without my permission. We have a project to finish. Let's not forget that!"

Just then the ground shook again and I had to grab hold of the table to keep from being thrown to the floor. This tipped the scales against Lo Sin. If it was a choice between a bullet in the head or drowning in the sea and being dashed against the rocks, everyone in the room was willing to risk the bullet for a chance to survive. Lo Sin's armed guards were the first ones out the door.

Lo Sin stood watching them desert him with a horrible look of dismay on his face. "Cowards!" he screamed at them as they all but trampled him to get out the door.

He grabbed one white-coated technician and tried to keep him from going. The man threw him off with a violent push. "Come back here," Lo Sin shouted after him in Chinese.

Finally, the room was empty but for Lo Sin and myself. I came up behind him and took him by the arm. He spun around and glared at me, his eyes narrowed with malice.

"Come on, Old Man," I said. "You'll have to answer charges when we get back, but it's better than dying like this."

"Leave me alone," he growled.

"But you don't—"

The ground heaved again and sent us both sprawling on the floor. Memory banks toppled and sparks of electricity from broken cables snapped in the air. I smelled ozone, then the noxious odor of burning vinyl plastic.

"Get up!" I told him. "It's starting to burn!"

"Unhand me!" he shouted back and pulled his arm free of mine. "I am staying," he said flatly.

We stared at each other for several seconds. Then the fumes started to make it difficult to breathe. I knew it would do no good to try and force him to go. I had no choice but to leave him there.

I bolted through the door out onto the white gravel. On the landward side of the courtyard part of the wall had caved in. Lab technicians and guards were scrambling over the rubble to safety. I was about to follow them, when I heard a faint call for help.

Twenty

The cry came from the main part of the house. I ran across the courtyard to the heavy iron door and threw myself against it. It opened only a few inches. A roof beam had fallen behind it, keeping it all but shut.

I rammed it again with my shoulder. It moved a fraction of an inch. Then I listened. The cry was insistent. Somewhere inside a woman was trapped.

I hit the door again and again. Still it wouldn't budge. My shoulder felt like I'd been beating down brick walls. Finally, I had one more go of it. I took a running start and hurled myself, regardless of how it hurt.

The roof beam rolled back and the door swung open, not far, but far enough.

Inside was havoc. The remodeling done was obviously not very strong. The upper floors had collapsed. Gaping holes in the entryway ceiling looked out on the starry night, and everywhere thick wooden beams lay splintered and twisted as though they were toothpicks. The air was thick with dust and the smell of fire.

I ran down hall after hall, looking in one room after another. I could still hear the cry, only fainter now, as though whoever was screaming was on the verge of giving up.

I came upon the tea garden room where Minamoto and I had talked. One whole wall had caved in and half the ceiling lay in the shrubbery. The tea house had been demolished and the plumbing mechanism as well—the reflecting pool was nothing but an empty hole. The air was hazy as it was everywhere else, but the electrical system still functioned. The flourescents glowed through the dust like a dotted line of light along the floor.

In the next room where I'd fought Benkei, the robot monk, the situation was similar. The artificial stream had overflowed its banks and the room was filling with water. On either side of the stream was a pile of wreckage where the footbridge had fallen.

In the next room the dragon had fallen on its side and the phony clouds had fallen off the wall. The cry had now become a soft sobbing, but the sound was clearer here. It was coming from the room with the moveable wall sections in it.

I dashed to the opening where I'd been almost squeezed to death a few hours earlier. The wall section that acted as a door was snapping open and shut like a giant pair of jaws. The computer had obviously gone berserk.

I watched it zip back and forth a few times and realized it was moving too fast for me to slip through. I was going to need something to hold it open. I found a piece of a beam fallen from the ceiling and carried it over. When the door snapped back to the open position, I wedged it in and it held.

Inside it was like a nightmare. Walls moved forward,

fell back, hallways telescoped out or truncated them-selves with amazing speed. And what was more, every-thing moved at once. It was like being in the middle of a huge working engine, at the mercy of its pistons and all its moving parts.

As I stood watching this activity, the wall in front of me suddenly leaped out and knocked me down. Then it retreated just as suddenly, only to make room for an attack from the wall behind. I scrambled out of its way on all fours and it collided with its brother with a crack like two wooden blocks being smacked together.

I jumped to my feet and began doing some broken field running. Every time I got penned in, I looked for a hallway in some direction just opening up. Then I'd dive for it, more than once just ahead of certain death between two on-coming walls.

This went on for two or three minutes, and I'd had several close escapes, when a section of wall to my left jerked itself back and I saw the figure of a young woman huddled on the floor crying. She was Japanese, wearing a white lab coat.

Obviously, she'd gotten caught in here and by some miracle had managed to avoid being crushed to death. But now she was exhausted and about to give up.

Unfortunately, seeing her and getting to her were two different things. Just as I ran for her, a wall shot be-tween us and cut us off. Then, while I was waiting for the interval in this deranged machine which would move aside the wall that separated us, the far end of the hall I was standing in descended on me and pushed me several yards away. It came on me so fast, I had to run out in front of it. This one herded me into another, but stopped just short of crushing me flat. Then two halls opened up on either side.

I could go either of two ways, but I'd lost track of the

girl. "Where are you?" I shouted in Japanese.

"Is someone there?" she yelled back in English.

Two walls slapped together, making a terrible clap of noise.

"Hold on, I'll find you," I shouted.

I ran down the hall that I thought was in the direction of her voice. Behind me the wall section closed with a slap. Then the hall, that had opened up so nicely, closed, with the wall in front of me barreling down on me like a locomotive, stopping just before it had run me into wallpaper. Then another hall opened up unexpectedly to my right.

"Get me out of here!" she screamed. She was near hysteria.

"Don't panic!" I shouted back.

I took this hall. It went for a short distance before it was cut short. But I was closer to her now, I was sure of it.

"Don't move," I yelled. "Stay where you are."

The wall in front of me fell away. She was standing just behind it, drawn there by the sound of my voice, her face as pale as her coat and her cheeks glistening with tears. She ran over and buried her face in my neck.

As I held her, I looked down and saw what had saved her from being ground to hamburger by these walls. A large chunk of plaster had fallen off the ceiling and stuck itself in the track in the floor along which the walls moved. It had acted like a doorstop, creating an island of safety in the midst of pandemonium.

"What's your name?" I asked.

"Riko." It was no more than a whisper in my ear.

"We're not out of here yet," I told her, pulling her away.

She nodded grimly.

"Can you run?" I asked.

Before she could answer, the end of the hallway plunged toward us and we were running, hand in hand, me pulling her along, until we ran out of room. Then the walls on either side suddenly split and we dived into the new hallway on the left as the old one closed with a powerful bang.

I helped her to her feet. "That was close," I said.

She just looked at me and smiled. She was too grateful to speak.

"The door is this way, I think," I told her, pointing to the wall on our left.

"I think so," she said.

"The trick is to stay out in front of these walls," I said. She nodded. "Don't worry. I'll be right here," I assured her.

The hall we were in started to close down and we had to move. There was no panic this time. An escape route opened up in front of us and we just stepped into it as the hall snapped shut behind us. It looked like getting out of here wasn't going to be all that difficult. That was, if I was right about the location of the door.

Then a yawing sound, like something enormous being wrenched apart, broke the air and the floor below us tilted ten degrees or more. We fell into each other, against the wall, and finally to the floor. The lights failed and the wall sections suddenly stopped moving.

"What's going on?" she said, terrified. "Why is it dark?"

"The house is falling into the ocean," I said.

"Into the ocean?" she said it as if she couldn't believe it.

"Didn't you hear that explosion a while ago? That was dynamite in the rock face under the house. It's undermined the integrity of the cliff. We're falling, although not as fast as I thought."

"You did it?"

"Minamoto and I, yes."

Outside, the house was breaking apart. More of the superstructure was falling into the lower rooms. Beams crashed, followed by a rain of plaster. Masonry hit the floor and vibrated the joists below us.

"We've got to get out of here." I grabbed her hand and together we began feeling the surface of the walls. I counted thirty steps until we found an opening. The opening was on the left, which was good, because left was the direction I thought the door was in.

The next hall over was a little longer. I counted forty-one steps, then we found a hall that went right, and from the sound of our voices, it went for quite a ways.

Riko wanted to take it. "Please, let's get out of here," she begged. "I'm getting scared. I keep thinking the walls are closing in on us again."

"This hall leads away from the door. We should only take those that lead to the left," I said, trying to sound positive about where the door was.

She acquiesced without a struggle and we continued on, me running my hand along the wall in the dark, hoping for an empty space that would lead us in the right direction.

Finally, I hit a long hall going left. When we turned into it, she asked, "Why is it so hot in here?"

"Fire. The house is on fire."

She didn't say anything, but gripped my hand tighter.

At the end of the hall I felt the crack of the door. The beam I'd wedged in it was still there, but the wall that moved back and forth against the door, the one that had almost crushed me my first time through this maze, was partially blocking the entrance. The opening that remained for the door was alarmingly small.

Riko went first, squeezing her small body into the crevice between the two walls. It took her several minutes of maneuvering, but she made it.

Then it was my turn. I took off Wilhelmina and her holster and handed them through to Riko. Then I removed the turtleneck sweater I'd taken off the guard and the belt from my pants. Then I started to squeeze through.

I got my arm, leg, shoulder, and part of my hip through, but I couldn't see how I'd make it any further. Then I sucked in for all I was worth and jammed in my shoulders and one buttock.

The yawing sound, like the creaking of a huge door, erupted again, and the house tilted. The two walls that held me in their grip suddenly closed the grip tighter. I screamed in pain. I thought my body would burst.

"Are you all right?" Riko asked anxiously.

I couldn't respond. The pain was immense, and I could hardly breathe. Every pulse brought on a new wave of agony.

Riko, not as frail as she looked, began to pull on me frantically, trying to wrest me free. It was hopeless. I was about to tell her to run on without me, when the house shifted again and the wall fell back. I slipped through the opening, then through the door where I'd wedged the beam, and none too soon. I'd just cleared it when the wall slammed shut, sealing the doorway for good.

She helped me up. I had trouble getting my legs to hold me. My body shook all over.

"I'm all right," I said, anticipating what she was about to ask.

"You're sure?"

"We haven't got time. We've got to make a run for it." I took a step and stumbled. She threw my arm around her neck and together we started to run.

Plaster and bits of stone and wood showered down on us from above. The house wrenched again in another throe of its demise, almost knocking us down.

We ran through the room past the carcass of the mechanical dragon to the door panel. She was about to run in, when I stopped her. She couldn't see very well through the darkness and the dust, but the water level in the next room had risen to twice what it was. The whole room was a vast swimming pool of floating debris.

We stepped in cautiously, keeping to what little dry ground we could find, which consisted of a raised patch by the panel opening. Riko looked at me a little doubtfully, as if to ask, "Do we have a choice?" Then she began to step into the water.

"Hold it," I said, grabbing her arm. There was a cable not far away that was still hot. Every now and then it lashed above the surface and spit out yellow sparks that lit the room. "Wait here," I said.

I went back into the other room, up to the body of the dragon. My sword with its insulated handle still protruded from his mouth. I pulled it out and took it back to where Riko was waiting. Then, inching along between the water's edge and the wall and leaning out as far as I could, I used the sword to guide the cable close enough for me to grab it by its insulation.

"There's no telling if that's the only one," I said, pulling the cable out and laying it on the bank.

"We'll have to take the chance," she answered. She went in first, wading until it got deep enough to swim. I followed. In a few minutes we reached the other doorway.

Then we ran, hand in hand, until we were clear of the house and in the courtyard. We were halfway across the open gravel when she stopped me.

"There's someone else," she said, pointing to the light in the window of the dust-free lab where they had been working on the duplicate.

"No," I said, "that's just—" But she'd pulled away from me and was running to the door of the lab.

It was getting too late, and there wasn't much time. A fissure had already opened in the ground underneath the courtyard. I hesitated for the briefest second, then ran after her.

We reached the door together.

"Don't open it," I said. "There's nothing in there of any importance."

She didn't listen. She pulled the door open. Through the glass panels on the other side of the waiting area Lo Sin was over the laboratory table, his back to us.

"It's the Master," she said. I pulled on her trying to stop her, but she shook her hand free.

She crossed the anteroom quickly almost to the big man's broad backside, then something she saw made her stop. I came up behind her and gently put my arms on her shoulders. Lo Sin was bent over the still-open face of his unfinished robot, vainly trying to stuff the components back into it, mumbling to himself in a run of unintelligible Chinese. Tears ran down his soaked cheeks and dripped off the edge of his jaw.

"He doesn't want our help," I told her quietly.

She stared for several seconds, then she, too, began to cry. Finally, I took her firmly by the arm and led her away.

Outside, the fissure had grown in size. From the way it was spreading, I could tell it was a matter of seconds before the entire lip of the cliff crumbled away.

By the time we got to it, it was almost too wide to jump. Riko stood on the edge of the giant crack, looking down. Then she looked at me with anguish.

"You have to jump," I said. "There's no other way."

"I'll never make it."

"You have to."

About fifteen feet of empty space separated the two banks of ground. "Make a run for it," I said, "and give it everything you've got."

Her eyes went white like an animal's when it's trapped. She looked around frantically, but there was no other means of escape. Still, she didn't move. It was like her feet had grown roots.

"Jump!" I screamed in her ear. "You're not going to give up on me now."

She looked at me again and seemed to come to her senses. She stepped back a few paces, ran and propelled herself into the air. She came down just short of the goal, hanging to the rock ledge by her hands for dear life, her feet dangling in the blackness.

Then it was my turn. I took a run and made it, without much room to spare. Quickly I grabbed her and pulled her up. Then a crash of thunder rumbled like a mountain being dropped.

I turned and saw an entire hundred yards of firm ground suddenly break, as though it had been struck off by a giant chisel, and slide into the dark sea. I pulled her up by the wrists and the two of us stood watching. It took many seconds for it to finally go.

Then we went up to the rocks on the other side of the courtyard wall where the lab technicians, guards, and other personnel were watching. The lot of us stared down at the wreckage of the house for some time.

Then a nice looking Japanese man in a white lab coat

spotted Riko and came running over. He grabbed her and swung her up in the air, jabbering excitedly. She clung to him with all her might. She was obviously very glad to see him. When he set her down, they kissed—a long, long kiss that made me smile.

When they were done, she broke free of him, ran to me, leaped up and kissed me, too. She looked at me as though she wanted to say something, but there was nothing to say. She just smiled and slipped out of my arms and ran to her young man. The two of them walked off arm in arm, and she began telling him of the time we had getting out.

I watched them go. The sun was beginning to rise and the eastern sky had turned to pastels. As I walked up to where I'd parked the Porsche, I remembered I was going to have to tell Gigi about her brother.

THE END

THE PUPPET MASTER

David Hawk, chief of AXE, the super secret action intelligence organization, left his office in the Amalgamated Press Building on Dupont Circle and climbed in the back seat of a plain gray sedan. Immediately the young naval officer eased the car away from the curb and they headed north along Connecticut Avenue across the Taft Bridge.

Hawk was a well built man in his early sixties. He had a thick shock of white hair, a broad, square face that seemed best suited for a scowl than a smile, and clenched in his teeth was an ever present cigar.

It was a cold, stone gray afternoon and a biting north wind that had blown for the past two days seemed to have put everyone in Washington, D.C. on edge, including Hawk who at this moment was a very worried man.

He had spent most of his life in service to his country, including the OSS during the War, the CIA when it was formed in the late forties, and finally the directorship of AXE which had been created during the McCarthy witchhunts that had effectively hamstrung many of the CIA's operations.

During those long years Hawk had observed the missions he had authorized, sometimes from his office, which was called the Ivory Tower behind his back, and sometimes from the field.

He had sweated over hundreds of operations whose

199

outcomes were doubtful from the very beginning. He had agonized over the occasional operation that had failed for one reason or another. And he had tried his damndest to explain the precise function that AXE played in the security of the free world to eight incoming Presidents.

During that time he had made some friends, but many more enemies. Hawk was the sort of person who never pulled his punches. He generally said what he thought when he thought it, and expected the same from the people around him.

As a result he was not a well liked man. But he was respected. His decisions were looked upon by his staff nearly as words of God. And every President so far, as well as the Joint Chiefs, held him in high regard.

On the other side of the coin, however, there were damn few men who had ever earned and then kept his respect. Among the few of them was Nick Carter. presently AXE's senior field man, who several years ago had earned the designation N3, Killmaster.

The driver turned off Connecticut Avenue onto Jones Bridge Road, breaking into Hawk's morose thoughts, and he looked up as they came through the back gate into the National Naval Medical Center compound and proceeded along a tree lined lane.

Six months ago Hawk had signed the mission authorization forms which had sent Nick Carter to this place. And now as the car approached the parking lot behind the Psychological Research Building, he wondered if he had signed Nick's death warrant as well. . . .

—From THE PUPPET MASTER
A new Nick Carter Spy Thriller
from Ace Charter in March